Marissa Rewritten

A Novella

Second Chance Series: Book I

Kyle Hunter

The Second Chance Series

In *The Second Chance Series*, you'll meet Marissa, Julia, Sydney, and Eden, four college friends who, twenty-five years later, renew their friendships as they find themselves empty nesters and single again. You'll love getting to know these women and following each one in her own book.

Marissa Rewritten   *(Book 1)*

Julia Redesigned   *(Book 2)*

More books by Kyle Hunter that will take you places

Circle Back Around

One December

Provence Series

Prodigals in Provence (Book I)

A Promise in Provence (Book II)

Chapter One

Marissa Thompson panned a critical glance across her dining room. She approached the cherrywood table, laden with china and crowned with a silk centerpiece, and tucked a loose blossom into place. Of course, the girls didn't care if they ate from paper plates or crystal. They weren't picky or prone to put on airs. Even less now than when they'd all been in college together a lifetime ago. Each of her three friends had been through too much in the last twenty-five years to worry about the little things.

Not that Marissa cared excessively about the little things or peoples' opinions, either. But she loved her historic Raleigh home with its carved banister, crown molding, and high ceilings. The long wrap-around porch so epitomized the south, the gardenia bushes along its length, releasing a gentle scent through open windows. The house represented her and spoke about what was important to her. And she was thrilled the reunion would take place that weekend in her home. She'd missed her friends. Julia. Sydney. Eden. She *needed* to see them. It had been a long year.

The phone pinged. Marissa dashed to the coffee table and checked the screen. A text message from Sydney. *Hey, Marissa. Just wanted to let you know I'll be there around five. Hit some construction traffic on 77 but nothing too bad. Can't wait to see you all!*

Marissa smiled at the tangible proof that they'd be together soon. Everyone was scheduled to arrive between five and six, coming to Raleigh from other cities and states. She'd prepared the food, the downstairs, their bedrooms. Everything was ready so she'd still have enough time to do some Facebook marketing. Bleh. Marketing wasn't her passion, but it was the least she could do for her fans and prospective readers of her historical fiction novels, in the place of giving them an actual book. Which she hadn't done in a while.

Her cell phone rang. She hoped it wasn't Eden or Julia saying they'd be late. Marissa had planned dinner at seven followed by a great weekend of lunching, shopping, laughter and catching up. She sank into the wing-back chair and reached for her phone on the side table. She saw the name "Randall" pop up and her heart sagged. Once again, she had nothing much to tell her agent.

"Hi, Randall. How was your vacation?" She kept her voice light and perky, hoping it was mostly a social call, knowing better.

"Fine, Marissa. Real good. Relaxing, which I needed. Did you get away?"

"Yes, to the beach for a few days last month before it gets too hot and crowded." She rubbed the brass rivets on the arm of the chair, her skin moist against the metal. "This weekend three college friends are coming for a reunion, so I'm looking forward to that. We've known each other for twenty-five years."

"That's good you've kept in touch with them all these years." His voice took on a strained thinness. Marissa tensed. Perspiration broke out on her neck.

"Marissa, this is hard to say, but I'm going to have to drop you as a client if you don't have a new story idea soon. I know it's been hard for you, losing Robert like you did, and I've tried to be patient."

A cold ripple shuddered through her. She'd expected this sooner or later. "Randall—" Her words emerged like sandpaper. "You've been more than patient with me." She cleared her throat, swallowed. "You've hung in there with me for over a year and I'm so grateful. But I—I hope you won't give up on me."

An audible sigh followed by two long seconds of silence on the line. Marissa heard a car rumble by outside, then another. A dog barked. Finally, Randall said, "Do you think you can come up with a story idea within a month? I can give you one month. Maybe a sequel to Joanna? It was such a popular novel and series and the books have done well."

Marissa nodded. The Joanna books had done well enough to keep her out of the poorhouse over the last year and a half that she hadn't written a thing. But her fans were losing patience, too. "I tried to create another adventure for Joanna, but really, I thought three books were enough for the series. Actually, I'd like to start a new series."

Randall paused. "Okay . . ." His voice sounded tentative, hopeful. "A new series would be *very* good. Do you think you can come up with a new idea within a month? And a loose outline for the first two books of the series within two? If you have an idea, I'll give you that time. But that's all I can do, Marissa."

She let out a breath. "Oh, thank you, Randall. Yes, yes, I'll have an idea by then. I know I'll have something. I needed time to grieve Robert, of course, but then I hit the doldrums. I couldn't get myself going again. But I think I'm much better now." Small exaggeration. Or wishful thinking.

"Okay." He sounded genuinely relieved now. He believed her.

Marissa bit her lip. Her hand felt slick on the cell phone. *Oh, Lord, don't let me be a liar. I want to do what I promised.*

If she couldn't, she'd end up with a very short writing career.

After she hung up, a heavy cloud crept in and overshadowed her mood. She stood and paced the living room once, twice. She stopped in front of a silver-framed photo of herself with Robert, both of them smiling into the camera on a carefree day of sunshine and possibilities. The dim and narrow world of her childhood and adolescence had burst into color when she met him. She could still picture him in freshman English class sitting two rows from her, his curly hair sticking out over his ears. And for over two decades he was the love of her life. When he died, everything returned to dim for a long time.

Not completely, though. There was her son, Sean, who lived in Atlanta and was getting established in his first job out of college. They talked or texted a few times a month. Occasionally, he'd visit. She had her house, which she and Robert had purchased when she received her first-ever sizable advance for the Joanna series. Then there was her writing career, which she loved. At that moment, it hung by a fine filament in danger of being severed. The muse had apparently escaped on a one-way flight without leaving a forwarding address.

She couldn't lose her writing career. Who would she be without it?

In the last ten years, she'd defied her mother's predictions of a small, dull life, one in which she worked shelving other peoples' books rather than writing her own. After she left for college, her world stretched out, pushing down the walls that had surrounded her all her life. She'd been a mousy adolescent at first, fearful of each day. But during the first year, she met Eden, Sydney, and Julia. And then Robert.

She couldn't go backward. She'd come too far. She had to come up with an idea for a new book. Had to.

Marissa prayed and pep-talked herself and by the time the doorbell rang at five fifteen, she'd managed to plaster a reasonable facsimile of a peaceful expression on her face. The prospect of the coming weekend nudged a portion of her discouragement to the back burner. Her *friends* were coming.

She hurried to the door and flung it open. Sydney stood there, a wide grin on her face, her willowy form casual in denim capris, a tank top, and flip-flops. She lived in Charlotte, so she knew how to dress for May in North Carolina. The two women squealed and wrapped each other into a hug.

"So good to see you!" Marissa ushered Sydney inside the house. She took the canvas tote from Sydney's hand and ducked into the kitchen to set it on the counter. "You can put your suitcase there in the foyer. I'll show everyone to their rooms later."

Sydney set a cloth-covered weekender bag down on the hardwood floor. "The bag there has some munchies for us, a couple bottles of wine, and a casserole for tomorrow." She stepped into the living room and her eyes panned the room. "Oh, your house is lovely! What year was it built?"

"1905."

"I love historic homes! And you have such a flair for decorating. Julia will love this." Sydney strolled through the living room and ran two fingers across the carved wooden mantle of the brick fireplace. She turned, arms crossed, and gazed at the ornate details and comfortable but elegant furnishings.

"Thanks, I love it here." Marissa felt a flush of pleasure at Sydney's admiration. She anticipated Julia's response, too, since she had a business in interior design. "There's a lot of upkeep, but for me, it's worth it. I'll have to do a couple of repairs this fall. One good thing is, the house is big enough for all of us to party away all weekend!" She forced a tone of celebration into her voice then gestured Sydney to follow her into the kitchen. "Come, we can talk in here."

Sydney followed Marissa to the kitchen and perched on a stool at the speckled gray granite island. "I *so* need this weekend away and being with you all. I'm just finishing my grades for the year after putting in a lot of extra hours. The kids have been antsy for almost a month. This time next week, I'll be done for the whole summer."

"I bet you can't wait." Marissa grinned and opened the fridge to place Sydney's casserole inside. She pulled out a frosty pitcher of chilled water with lemon slices floating on the surface, poured it into two glasses, and set one of them in front of Sydney. "Last time we all met, you said you were thinking of leaving teaching to do something else. Any more thoughts on that?"

Sydney waved the air dismissively. "Oh, I go through that about every three months or so. I'm sure one day I'll really do it. I'll resign from teaching and do something completely unrelated."

"You'll know when that time comes." Marissa sat across from Sydney. "I admire you. You're so committed to your students, even the tough ones. On top of that, you're so smart with numbers. I don't have a mathematical bone in my body. I'm only good at words, that's it. Though, not too much lately." She leaned on the other side of the island and glanced over Sydney's head through the kitchen window, feeling the weight of her own words.

Sydney leaned forward on folded hands. "I love your words, Marissa. I, along with everyone in America and maybe England too, loved the Joanna series. I hated for that last book to end. You are *so* gifted." She paused and caught Marissa's gaze. Her voice softened. "Though I know lately it hasn't been easy." She reached out and grasped Marissa's hand.

The simple gesture brought a sting to Marissa's eyes. She squeezed back and blinked, following with an awkward smile.

"You're right. It's been hard to get myself re-motivated after—after Robert. I can always find things to distract me. I've enjoyed working in the garden. I took a painting class. It was as though I wanted to avoid writing, even though I love it. I'm not sure what was going on inside." She'd better figure it out fast. She wouldn't mention the call with Randall, which was still too raw.

"You were healing, Marissa."

Yes, that and a good dose of inertia.

Sydney pulled her thick ash-brown hair behind her shoulders and took a gulp of cold water. She could have easily been a model instead of a high-school math teacher. Her passionate stories of her low-income students gave ample evidence of her dedication to them. That explained her persistence in her sometimes-difficult profession.

"What time is everyone getting here?"

"I expect them before six. Eden flew into Dulles last night from Indianapolis and she's driving here with Julia."

"Then we'll be complete."

Marissa took a deep breath. "Yes, complete."

Two hours later Marissa, Sydney, Julia, and Eden sat around the dining room table, ready to dive into the feast Marissa had prepared. Flickering candles cast a golden hue across the table. China dinner plates brimmed with chicken cordon bleu, fingerling potatoes sautéed in butter and herbs, and steamed asparagus in hollandaise sauce. Enticing aromas of sautéed potatoes and chicken circled around the table.

"This looks fabulous, Marissa. We told you not to go to any trouble." Julia leaned forward, but despite her gentle admonition, her face showed delight and anticipation as she took a sniff of the steaming homemade biscuits.

Marissa looked around the table at her friends. Julia, with her Mediterranean complexion and dark hair, Sydney, the tall and athletic, and Eden, a petite blonde with a bubbly, outgoing personality. They were all so attractive while Marissa considered herself rather plain. At least she wasn't the jealous kind. She knew Robert had considered her beautiful and talented. She tried to draw comfort from that. Occasionally, she attempted to see herself the way Robert saw her. She was still working on that skill. It was much harder without him there to remind her.

She turned back to Julia and smiled. "I wanted to do something special for our first evening back together."

"I'm so happy that we've managed to keep our reunions, though with our schedules, I know it's not easy." Eden glanced around the table for signs of agreement. "We need to do our best to keep our dates with each other."

"I vote for a cruise next time." Sydney lifted her water glass. "Any takers?"

"Either that or a long weekend in San Francisco," Marissa said.

"I'm sure we'll have lots of ideas. But the main thing before we leave here is to get out our calendars and schedule our next one, okay?" Eden's round, blue eyes invited a response.

A chorus of agreement resounded from around the table. "I know we sort of kept in touch in a sketchy way after college with Christmas cards, Facebook, the occasional Skype visit—" began Julia.

"Better than nothing." This from Eden.

"Thank goodness for technology!" Sydney said.

"Amen to that." Eden looked back at Julia. "Finish your statement, Julia. We're sorry to be rude friends who interrupt."

Julia laughed. "That's okay. I wanted to say that even though we've kept only loosely in touch over the years, I find it so rare and wonderful that we've made a commitment at this point in our lives to see each other regularly and get together twice a year."

The other women murmured their agreement.

"Through the years and the trials and the careers and kids—" Julia shook her head, hands splayed.

"And husbands—" added Eden with a chuckle.

"Oh, yes, the husbands. Well, we won't talk too much about them. That's rather a sore subject for all of us." Sydney smirked and reached for the potatoes.

"— here we are, twenty-five years later. We have a lot of history among us and I feel so blessed to be here with you all." Julia's voice softened as she finished her thought and looked around the table. "And now so much has changed for every one of us. Now, we're—" she hesitated, one hand gesturing in the air.

"Post-married." Sydney's statement brought laughter followed by a few seconds of solemn silence.

"Yeah," said Eden. "We're single. Who would have thought, ten or even fifteen years ago, that all four of us would be sitting here post-married?"

"Better than dead, I guess," Sydney said. The laughter was more muted.

"Just goes to show you how surprising life can be," Marissa said quietly as a trace of sadness swelled inside her. "Some of you went through awful divorces and others of us have lost our husbands. We never expected these things."

"But we're strong," said Eden emphatically. "God gets us through it, whether death or divorce. And we survive. We get stronger. And here we are together, supporting each other. This is only our second reunion, but we'll have many more. I'm sure of it." Eden's face shone with certainty and contentment. She'd been widowed for nearly ten years. Now she had the ability to talk about her husband without tearing up or feeling the wave of desolation mount up inside. At one time, she'd walked in Marissa's shoes. She, too, had gone through the daily struggle to get out of bed and keep living.

Eager to change the subject, Marissa turned to Eden. "Eden, how is your restaurant going?"

The candlelight glinted off of Eden's sleek shoulder length haircut, making it shine like polished brass. "It's going well, thanks to my brilliant chef. Wish I'd hired him years ago. Actually, I'm considering selling. I'm tired of the restaurant business and a couple people have shown interest in buying it."

"Oh, keep us posted," Julia said. "What will you do next?"

"No idea." Eden gave them a hesitant grin followed by a shrug. "Maybe I'll travel or write a cookbook. Or both. Or maybe I'll move, leave Indiana. It wasn't my choice to live there in the first place, but there I am, fifteen years later." Eden sighed. For a moment all mirth dropped from her face and a shadow crossed her brow. "I'll let you know what I end up doing once I know that myself." Her smile returned as she glanced around the table.

"I think you should move to North Carolina," said Julia. "Or northern Virginia or Maryland, near me. D. C. is nearby and *quite* exciting."

Marissa took the platter of chicken and passed it for a second round.

"At least move to a place where we can get together more easily and often." Marissa was relieved that the conversation had moved on. "Raleigh, for example." They all laughed.

"Here, here." Sydney lifted her wineglass. "Charlotte would work, too."

Eden leaned forward and placed her elbows on the table. "I'll keep you all posted. Sounds like I have plenty of potential destinations. I'll definitely need your advice when the time comes, so you might be sorry you asked."

"No problem, you can count on us to tell you everything we think you should do with your life," Sydney said. A new round of laughter followed.

"And what about you, Julia? You haven't filled us in on your life yet or your business." Eden reached for the water carafe and served herself. "Anyone for a water refill?" She glanced around the table and refilled Sydney's glass.

Marissa couldn't read the expression on Julia's face but predicted bad news.

Julia leaned back in her chair. "I have some interesting clients. There's one guy who owns a small airline. He is having me redesign his whole first floor. That's kept me busy. He'd also like me to marry him."

This drew laughter and oohs. "Any potential?" Eden lifted her eyebrows.

Julia grinned and shook her head. "Along with that, I have some hotel clients, which I enjoy. The design store is doing pretty well. But I've had to cut back my time there because my mother has been getting worse. I'm the only child, so I need to be more available to visit her and take care of her needs."

"Anything new with her condition?" asked Marissa. "Or is it the same, just worse?"

Julia nodded, frowning. "Yes, it's the same, emphysema and Alzheimer's. Bad combination. It's hard to run a business and also be involved in her care to the degree I need to. But I have some great employees and assistants. That's made it easier to go see her. I just take it day by day." She let out a heavy sigh.

"Let us know if you need to talk or get away or anything, okay? We're here for you." Eden gave Julia a light squeeze on her arm.

Julia returned a small smile that didn't reach her eyes and said no more. The women fell silent.

After a moment, Eden turned to Marissa. "Marissa, aside from being a divine hostess, you've been quiet this evening. Is everything okay in your world?"

Marissa looked around at her friends and knew she was in a safe place to tell them about her current pressure. She sighed.

"Uh-oh, I knew it. You can tell us, Rissi." Eden's brow furrowed as she awaited Marissa's response.

Eden had walked with Marissa through becoming a widow. She was Marissa's closest friend among them, although Marissa loved them all like sisters and considered them all her best friends. If there was one place she could be transparent, it was there. "This is very recent news, like, this afternoon recent, so don't be mad because I didn't tell you all sooner. My agent, Randall, said he'd have to drop me if I didn't give him an idea within a month."

A collective gasp echoed around the table.

"That's cruel!"

"How could he?"

"Doesn't he know what you've been through?"

Marissa held up one hand. "Actually, he's stood by me for the last year and a half. He's given me time, but I haven't given him anything. At all. Not in a year and a half since Robert's death." She frowned and her shoulders sagged. "A man's got to earn a living. He's been compassionate, but there are limits. He's in demand as an agent, so I get it." She finished with a shrug.

"Yeah, I can see that." Julia's voice lost its indignation.

"What will you do?" asked Sydney.

"I told him I'd have an idea within a month and an outline for two books of a series within two."

Julia's eyes widened with her smile. "That's great. What's the idea?"

"I loved the Joanna books." At Sydney's statement, the other women echoed their agreement.

"That's just it, I don't have an idea. I'm finished with the Joanna series and I'm clean out of ideas. I'm trusting God to give me one within a month."

"You can do it, Marissa," Julia said. "You have a proven track record."

Marissa returned a forced smile, appreciative of their confidence. They didn't know she'd tried for months to come up with a new story that she could be interested in or better, excited about. She'd come up empty for months at a time.

"The Joanna series took place in Victorian England," Eden said. "Could you go back to England and let some history and culture seep in to give you more ideas?"

Marissa sighed. "I'd love to, but I don't have the money to go back. I went there with Robert before writing the Joanna series and everything just fell into place, the story, the sequels. I guess he was my muse."

"You could do U. S. history, then. The Gold Rush, the Civil War, the Revolution, the Colonies." Sydney rattled off her ideas and a chorus of agreement sounded from around the table.

That might work if only she could just develop an interest in some period of U. S. history for her historical novels. There were many monumental events in United States history. But her niche had always been Victorian England and it was hard to change continents and cultures to something entirely different. She may just have to. She'd been riding on Joanna's popularity for far too long.

Marissa and her friends finally went to bed at one-thirty. She climbed into her soft four-poster bed and let the day's exhaustion roll over her. Felt good to dissolve into the soft mattress. Though her body was comfortable and she was content with the evening, in the backdrop her thoughts were unsettled. She murmured another prayer about her dilemma. Her faith was weak on that subject.

She turned her head to gaze through the filmy curtains where she could see an almost full moon. It lit up the room with a soft, milky light. The sight was a comfort to her. She'd take her mind off of Randall's ultimatum for now, but eventually, she'd have to commit everything she had to finding a solution.

Chapter Two

Jarrod Lambert leaned back in his brown leather chair as his gaze drifted to the large picture window alongside his desk. At that moment, two tiny red birds were trying to peck their way into his home office through the glass. He smiled and leaned forward. When they saw him, they disappeared in a flash of red. Beyond the window, the late spring foliage in the yard of his Asheville, North Carolina home was distracting in its flowering beauty. Or maybe he was simply distracted that day.

Working at home had its benefits, like staying in stocking feet or slippers all day. Like taking a short nap after lunch or throwing in a load of laundry. It also had its disadvantages. Namely, reminders everywhere. Reminders of Rachel.

It hadn't been long after they'd finished the house, a sprawling modern yet historic-looking home he'd designed himself and had built. He and Rachel had just begun getting along better after a few years of on-and-off tension. He'd moved his architecture practice to the house and they saw each other more, developed a new rhythm of being around each other. It had been a sort of springtime renewal in their relationship. Then she was gone.

Now the house that they'd shared together was a hollow expanse filled with comfortable, tastefully-combined furnishings. It was a home before and now it was something like a hotel. He was still there most of the time, but it had lost its heart. It had lost Rachel.

Jarrod sighed. Two years trudged by and he'd gone on. Like a wounded man limping along then gradually straightening up. He was okay now. On most days. But those days still seemed rather pointless.

He scooped up and stacked blueprints and piles of content he couldn't recall. As he did, his eye caught the photo of Seth next to one of himself with Rachel. He sighed and reached for the photo. Time to put it away instead of letting it remind him of his failings as a brother. He slipped the framed picture of Seth into the bottom drawer of his desk, a cluttered space that rarely saw the light of day.

Too much pain. Too many losses. Too much unsaid.

Jarrod stood. He'd stop early that day. It was almost time to stop anyway, and his mental distractions were taunting him. He'd been thinking about Bethany a lot lately. Missing her. Or missing what they used to have together. His and Rachel's only daughter was just about to finish her third year of college at UNC Wilmington. She'd been physically out of the house for three years but he feared her spirit had slipped even further out of his reach, especially after losing her mother.

It was only four-twenty, but maybe he could catch her between classes or exams. He sat back down and slid his cell phone across the desk toward him. Dialed her number.

"Hey, Dad." Her voice sounded sleepy. "I'm surprised to hear from you."

"Hey, Sweetie. You sound tired. Everything alright?" Jarrod thrummed his fingers on the wood surface of his desk.

"Yeah, everything's fine. I stayed up most the night to study for a final I had this morning, so I had to take a nap. Just woke up a few minutes ago." As if to underscore her point, she let out a noisy yawn.

"How did your exam go?"

"I don't know. I'm just glad it's over. One down, three to go. Then I'm done."

"Great. I'm sure you'll do fine." Had they discussed her summer plans? Yes, he'd tried to broach it once and she hadn't known. In fact, she'd seemed evasive. "After your exams, will you be home? At least for a visit?"

Pause. "Um, I don't think so. I've lined up a job at a restaurant. I want to stay here this summer. The beach'll be great and some of my friends are staying here too."

Disappointment pooled in his chest, feeling like a metal weight hitting bottom. "Not even a brief visit home after your exams? To see your old man?"

"I'd love to, but I need to start this job right after exams are over. In fact, my first night of training is a couple of days *before* my last final. That won't give time to drive all the way back home."

"I'd really love to see you, Bethany. It's been since Christmas." It was on the tip of his tongue to say *I need to see my little girl.* He didn't want to pressure her. Yes, he missed her, but also had a mounting sense that they were on two separate icebergs drifting apart from each other.

"Yeah, it's been a while. I'm sorry, Dad. I'd like to see you too."

As she spoke a shadow of an idea formed in his mind. "What if I came to see you? I could stay for a long weekend, or even a week." He needed a break and a drive to Wilmington might prove to be a refreshing change of pace. The beach, the Riverwalk, the history and charm of the town. And he'd get to see Bethany, to try to preserve, or rather, reconstruct, the closeness they'd had when she was a child.

"Um, that would be great, Dad. I will have to work, though, so can't spend all my time with you."

"Of course, I don't expect you to spend *all* your time with me. I'd love to see you, though, and you can work me in around your work schedule, okay? I can occupy myself with architecture research, things like that. Plus, it'd be a sort of vacation for me. What do you think? After your exams?"

"Sure, that'll be great. I'll have my last final this Wednesday, so any time after that. Just let me know your dates."

"Yes, I will, Sweetheart. I won't get in your way too much, but I hope you'll spend some time with me."

"No worries, Dad." Jarrod liked the way her voice spiked a bit at the end of her phrase, which he wanted to interpret as a lilt of enthusiasm at the idea of his visit. It was a good idea, to visit and enjoy the town. It might pull him out of his lethargy.

His work was going well, so that wasn't the problem. He'd had a sense for the last couple of months that he needed something exciting, something he could hope for, look forward to. He wasn't sure what it was, had prayed for direction, but so far was still restless and unanchored. Maybe he was simply lonely.

He loved some of the architecture in Wilmington that dated back to the Civil War era and even the Revolution. Why couldn't he get a few ideas there to incorporate into his practice, instead of yielding to the current trend of giant multi-colored shoe boxes for apartment buildings and cookie-cutter mini-mansions for single-family dwellings? He could take in a couple of tours to feed his love of history. He'd read volumes about Civil War battles, the ironclad ships, the blockade-runners. There were historic sites all around Wilmington, so if he had extra time, he could always scout them out. Maybe play a little golf. He'd make the most of his visit.

Jarrod pulled himself back out of his chair and felt a new lightness in his step. Not that one week in Wilmington would change his world, but at least he had something to look forward to.

Changing his environment would be a help. Being with his daughter would do even more.

Since losing Rachel, the gap separating him from Bethany had become more painful and the object of fervent prayers. Seeing and spending some time with her on her turf might start a gradual process of closing that gap.

ભ ભ ભ

Tuesday morning, Marissa stood on the front porch with Eden. She didn't want to say goodbye to her friend, but Eden's taxi waited at the curb to take her to the airport. "I could have driven you, you know. The airport isn't that far."

Eden simply smiled and pulled Marissa toward her for a final hug. "Thank you for everything! Your book is going to come together, I just know it. Keep me posted." She pulled away and slung her weekend bag over one shoulder. In the other hand, she took the handles of a large canvas bag. With a wave, she crossed the lawn toward the cab. Soon, the vehicle disappeared from sight.

Marissa sighed and shuffled into the kitchen straight to the coffee pot. She'd already shared a cup with Eden, who'd stayed an extra day after Julia and Sydney left. The one-on-one time nourished different but equally important needs inside her.

Her eyes felt heavy inside her skull. She measured two scoops of coffee into the small pot. Despite her well-earned fatigue, the memory of her weekend with the girls brought a smile to her lips. She shoved Randall's words into a dim crevice in her mind. Added a third scoop of coffee.

Her weekend had been the perfect escape from her current life. She and her friends had stayed up late, curled up on the couches in their pajamas like teenagers at a sleepover. They reminisced about their naïve and hopeful college days and the years that had unfolded afterward. They wove webs of future dreams, ate and drank with abandon (the diets were postponed to a more convenient time.) There were restaurants and window shopping, then one afternoon at the Raulston Arboretum to enjoy the May flowers. For months she'd needed that emotional sustenance of just being together with her friends.

But it was over until their next get-together, scheduled near Thanksgiving. Now she must face her life again. She leaned forward and breathed in the nutty smell rising from her cup. The coffee would help her grope her way through her mental fogbank. Then she'd have to handle Randall's ultimatum.

If that weren't enough of a burden, she needed to get a few repairs done in her house, most of which she'd put off for fear of the price tag. But deferred maintenance would only cost more later, as her brother Clive the contractor had always told her. He didn't miss the opportunity to say it again just the other day as she tried to sweet-talk him into putting her tasks on his calendar. At least they'd overcome the minor feud they'd had just after their mother's death. During that period two years earlier, Marissa felt he'd left most of their mother's care—and looking after her estate—to her. He never owned up to his negligence and she tired of waiting for that admission, so she let it go.

Water under the bridge. Now more than ever, since she needed him. The wall in her kitchen had developed cracks and had to be repaired. It wasn't an emergency but the sight of it irritated her each morning when she'd look around her perfectly-decorated kitchen. The upstairs bathroom was another story. She knew there was some mold behind the wallpaper that had to be dealt with and she'd have Clive change the tile while he was at it, since the flooring had gotten uneven. If she got her idea for Randall, she'd ask her brother to change the vanity at the same time.

If she didn't, she'd probably have to sell her house. The thought made her stomach clench.

Coffee in hand, Marissa wandered into the living room, which was still in need of a good cleaning after the weekend. Despite that, it was one room that was pristine in beauty and detail. The built-in sculpted white bookshelves held an artful arrangement of decorative pieces and books. *Her* books were among them. The Joanna books stood together, spines outward, like a trophy. She stood motionless and stared at them, special hardback versions with faux leather covers. She tried to draw strength from the sight. After all, she'd written these. Surely, she could do it again.

Lord, give me an idea like you did for the Joanna series. I need inspiration. Her heart whispered, pleaded. Her spirits slipped.

"You've got to rattle the cage, Marissa! Don't sleep in it, for pity's sake!"

Marissa's head jerked back slightly then she smiled. Just like something Joanna would say. Joanna's words were deep in Marissa's head, with her refined British accent and her unrelenting spunk. Not surprising that her words would pop out just then when Marissa most needed them. Joanna would know how much Marissa craved some encouragement at that very moment.

"How do I rattle the cage, Joanna?" Her words broke the silence in the house. "How?" The word emerged in a whisper. Yet she knew she had been sleeping in a cage of her own making. She sighed. "I'll do it. I will rattle the cage *today.* You hold me accountable. I need your successor and I need her *now.*"

Joanna's prompting led Marissa to shower then spend an hour and a half surfing for ideas by pulling up historical articles of events around the world. Interesting, but lacking that special trigger she was seeking. Afterwards, her spirits sagged again and she ended up gardening and cleaning out a closet. For a break, of course. Which would make her more creative later, right?

The day unfolded and Marissa stayed busy. She spoke with Clive, who agreed to stop by on Saturday. She cleaned the house and the bathrooms, did the sheets, the kitchen. She wasn't avoiding, she'd just had company for the weekend and needed to clean. Of course.

By evening her previous discouragement had grown a double layer, since she hadn't returned to her novel brainstorming after her break. As her mood darkened, Marissa opened the fridge and slid out the glass plate containing the remains of the chocolate cream pie that Julia had brought. She started to cut herself a slice but then decided to bring the entire Pyrex pie plate and a fork into the den. She placed the pie onto the ottoman, flopped on the couch, and grabbed the remote. She navigated to her favorite channel, the History Channel.

Tonight's episode was on the Civil War. She'd try to get interested in that period. Keep an open mind, as Sydney had suggested. It might be a suitable backdrop for a new series. The program piqued her interest so she kept watching. Within minutes she was absorbed by the drama of Civil War events in North Carolina. Wilmington was a strategic city during the war, with its burgeoning population and railroad lines. It also had the Cape Fear River, which contained an important port that had to be defended.

Maybe this was it. Maybe she could get inspired by events in Wilmington during the Civil War. Wilmington was only a two-hour drive from Raleigh, so on-site research would be easy and affordable. Despite the empty pie plate that stared back at her, Marissa felt a flicker of something new she hadn't felt in a while.

Hope. Maybe she could change directions and instead of Victorian England, write a series in Civil War North Carolina.

"Now, there you go, Marissa. Heading up a different road isn't so bad, is it? There's more you haven't discovered yet, and your readers as well. Wouldn't you agree?" Joanna's voice again rang clear in Marissa's mind.

"I guess so, Joanna. I've written about your world, but here's a whole *new* world and its events I could write about."

She smiled. She liked hearing Joanna guide her, much like Robert had guided her in the past. Robert had been her muse. He'd given her the confidence to write in the first place a few years after their son, Sean, had started school.

Before meeting Robert, her mother's voice had been the anti-muse circulating in her head when she wanted to attempt something new. "Do something you can handle, Marissa. Don't get all full of hair-brain ideas. Be a secretary or do library work. Just make sure it's steady income. That's the most important thing, since you'll likely need to support yourself."

Her mother meant well in her own condescending way. But dreaming big was never an option for Marissa. Robert had opened her mind to her own dreams and had accompanied her through her self-doubt.

Joanna's words returned to her then. Marissa had considered Victorian England to be her bailiwick, and it was. But there *was* more to discover. In Wilmington. And she had nothing to lose.

If she could create a compelling female character like Joanna, the pieces might fall into place. Joanna was feisty, confident. She went against the tight-laced culture of her day. She had all of the courage, persistence, and assertiveness that Marissa lacked.

After cleaning up the pie plate and turning off the lights and television, Marissa prepared for bed, but her mind was sifting and darting to Civil War facts and dates she'd heard on the program. Yes, she'd go that direction. American history, Civil War. In addition to giving her a setting she could research and develop, a totally different country and period in history could expand her readership. She wouldn't be typecast as an author who only wrote about Victorian England.

She climbed into her four-poster bed and reached to turn off her cell phone. On impulse, she decided to email her friends. They'd be thrilled at her decision.

Good evening, my dearest ladies. I trust you all made it home safely and have the same glow that I have from our wonderful weekend together. It was wonderful— No, she'd already used the word "wonderful". A good writer wouldn't do that. *—it was rejuvenating to see you all again!* That was completely true.

Thank you all for your suggestions and prayers for my series idea. I think I've made some progress tonight and wanted to let you all know. I've decided to do a new series during the Civil War era and the first book will take place in Wilmington. Thanks to you all, I am open to changing countries, which creates endless possibilities!

Marissa pictured the faces of each of her friends, missing them already. She'd likely get a response from at least two of them the following day. As she fluffed her pillows and reached for the switch on the bedside lamp, a ping sounded from her phone. Someone must still be up. She glanced at the phone's screen and a smile curled her lips. Eden had responded by text.

From Eden: *I knew it wouldn't take long. You were so worried, but I never was. You were blocked by Robert's death and now you're breaking through to the next part of your exciting life! What will you do next?*

Before Marissa had a chance to respond, another ping. Sydney. *That's great, Marissa! You're off to a great start. We're praying for ya. Keep us posted, please.*

Marissa texted Sydney a quick *Will do. I'm thinking of spending a long weekend or possibly longer in Wilmington as a first step. It's close and there's a lot of history there.* Then she texted a similar message to Eden.

From Eden: *That's a good idea. It's close, like you said. I haven't studied the Civil War much myself, but I'm sure I'll know a lot by the time I read your book! When are you going to Wilmington?*

Marissa responded, *Not sure yet, within a week or two. Thanks for your confidence, Eden. I miss you already! Sleep well, my friend.*

She turned off the phone then the lamp. Her eyes adjusted to the dark room and she could see the outline of the antique carved chest underneath the window. A veil of contentment stole across her as she lay on her back in the murky shadows of the room. She hadn't felt that in so long.

The peaceful moment split and vanished when she heard a thump downstairs. Her body tensed for a moment. She listened. Nothing more. Slowly, she relaxed. It was probably just a book or something falling over. Had she left anything on the kitchen table that could have fallen? That's likely all it was.

Her eyes became heavy. She should probably go down to investigate, but was afraid to. And in any case, it was only something that had fallen. No more noises followed. Just hazy thoughts of the Civil War and her trip to Wilmington flitting around in her mind as she drifted off to sleep.

Chapter Three

Marissa awoke the following morning and made her way downstairs. Wooden steps beneath her feet groaned, bringing a smile to her lips. At times like that, she liked to think that her old house was talking to her. Over the years she'd imagined she had a relationship with it. Especially since Robert's death.

The gentle blanket of hope that had enveloped her the night before still hovered around her. She had the first piece of the puzzle for her next book. Of course, she still needed the idea itself, but this was the furthest she'd gotten in almost two years. She'd visit Wilmington within a couple of weeks. She could stay in a cute, historic bed and breakfast. It would be like a mini-vacation and inspiration trip combined.

The sky out the front window was already a cloudless cornflower blue, which only lifted her spirits higher. Until she walked into her kitchen.

She let out a screech and her hands flew to her mouth. Part of her ceiling lay in a heap in the floor. *That* was the thud she'd heard the night before. She lifted her eyes to the source where an ugly two-foot hole gaped at her. She couldn't actually see the bathroom upstairs but some rotten wood beams were exposed. It was Wednesday and Clive wasn't scheduled to come by until Saturday.

Marissa needed him *now*.

She paced back and forth in the kitchen, carefully stepping over the debris. It was too early to call Clive but she wouldn't be able to focus on anything else until she gave him the news of her current crisis.

Eight-thirty wasn't too early to call Sydney, though. She was level-headed and would have calming advice. Or better, Julia. As an interior designer, she'd have some ideas.

The phone rang several times. When voice mail picked up, Marissa said, "Hi Julia. Just wanted to ask a word of advice on some house repairs. Maybe you've seen a variety of, um, situations in your work. Besides that, it's a good excuse to hear your voice! Hope you made it back home safely and I'll be praying for your mom." She hung up. Paced the room again.

She crossed her arms and took a deep gulp of air. Dialed Sydney's number. Voice mail. Sydney wasn't finished with her school year yet, so of course, she wouldn't answer. She was likely preparing her year-end grades or giving a final exam at that very moment.

It would have been so nice to have a voice on the other end of the line, someone soothing to tell her everything would be okay. Clive wasn't going to do that.

She was absolutely sure.

A half hour later, her phone rang. Julia, thank goodness. "Hi, Marissa. I only have a couple minutes, but what's going on down there?" Her voice sounded breathless. Marissa heard voices speaking and shouting in the background.

"Hey, Jules!" Marissa's voice was falsely upbeat. "Just—um—" Marissa swallowed a near flood of tears that rose in her throat. It would be okay. Julia would have an idea. "My house has some serious issues." She forced a chuckle. "A piece of the ceiling fell down in the kitchen."

"What? Oh, that's terrible, Marissa. It looked fine when we were all there just last weekend."

"Yes, well, fine on the outside. It chose today to crash down. I guess I should be grateful it didn't happen over the weekend." Marissa thrummed her fingers on the dining room table where the women had sat just a few days earlier. "My brother's a contractor. He's stopping by soon to look at it. I mostly needed a friendly voice. But if you have any ideas from a design perspective, that would be nice too."

After a "hmm" and a long pause, Julia said, "I'm so sorry, Marissa. I don't know much about the construction side of things. I wish I could help. Once your brother diagnoses the cause, I might have something useful to tell you."

"It's okay. I was just discouraged and created a pretext to call you." That was the real truth. Marissa hadn't really expected Julia to offer a practical suggestion outside her area of expertise.

"You don't ever need a pretext to call, my silly friend!" Julia scolded gently and followed with quiet laughter. So Julia. Even her good-natured teasing was genteel and soft. A wave of comfort subdued Marissa's despondency. "What about your novel? You said you had a new idea."

"Yes, I do. I just hope I can pull it off. I'm starting to feel like I did freshman year of college. Nervous and inadequate. Remember that?"

"Of course, I do. You blossomed after that."

"Having such good friends helped."

"We can't take credit, though we did see more potential in you than you saw in yourself."

Marissa sighed. "I feel a bit afraid of becoming that girl again."

"That's not even possible, Marissa. You were scared of your shadow then. Twenty-five years later, you are one hundred percent different. You're more confident, more anchored now."

Julia's voice was firm, certain. Marissa wasn't sure her insides matched the person she projected even to her closest friends. "I hope you're right. I guess I'm down because of, well, everything that's happened. I'm also missing all of you after such a wonderful weekend. It's a letdown, but I'll be fine. Tell me, how are *you*, Jules? We saw each other just a few days ago, but we didn't get to really talk, not with all of us there at once." Julia had seemed troubled the first night of the girlfriends' weekend.

Julia let out an audible sigh. "Oh, the same. It's just exhausting, running back and forth from my office to clients then to Mom's facility, then back to the office. Not sure how a hamster feels, but I think I can guess."

"I'm sorry. I know she appreciates your presence, though. She must sense it, even if she isn't sure—"

"—sure who I am? Yes, she's often not sure who I am. She gives me a sweet smile and tells me it was nice meeting me. That's—that's really hard for me, but I'm trying to accept it. She was a good mom for so many years. I'm her only child, so I try to look out for her, regardless." She paused. "I didn't mean to talk about me. You're the one with the crisis."

"I asked *you*. Anything upbeat happening? I'd like you to keep talking about you because I want to know. Also, it keeps my mind off my ceiling that's lying at my feet."

Julia laughed. "I shouldn't laugh. But there's something comical hearing you say that. Well, remember the client who wants to marry me? He offered to fly me to New York for dinner. You may recall he owns an airline."

"I love it!" Marissa couldn't help but chuckle. It felt good, lightening the heavy weight she felt against her chest. "Are you going to go?"

"I don't know. I don't want to lead him on, but he's rather persistent. I keep telling him I don't date my clients. Then he tells me it's not a date. It's just dinner."

"Whatever. Go, have fun. You deserve some fun, don't you?"

"Yes, and so do you. Maybe you can leave for Wilmington ahead of schedule."

Marissa leaned back on her heels and avoided looking around her kitchen. "I think I won't have a choice."

Chapter Four

Marissa stood outside the Beauford Bed and Breakfast in Wilmington for a moment and set her suitcase down on the brick sidewalk. She'd seen the historic home online, with its soft yellow siding, white trim, and ornate cupola on the roof. In person, it was even more charming, from its wrap-around porch endowed with wicker rocking chairs to the plush ferns hanging from the eaves. She mounted the brick steps and entered the establishment.

"Hello." She approached the young woman behind the counter, suddenly self-conscious. "I have a reservation under the name *Thompson*."

"Welcome to the Beauford." The young woman smiled then turned to face the computer screen. "Thompson. Here you are. Mrs. Marissa Thompson."

Marissa winced. She'd often wondered if she should drop the "Mrs". Not that she was in the market for a new Mr., but it was a reminder of what she had been. The wife of a wonderful man. For over two decades. Maybe the young woman wondered why Marissa was there alone. She'd never removed her wedding and engagement rings. Saw no reason to, and they helped her feel connected to Robert.

"Yes, that's correct." Marissa looked around her as the young woman tapped on her computer keyboard. Light ochre walls contrasted with dark wood beams and moldings around the doors and windows, giving the place an early American look. A glance into the next room revealed a sitting room with wing-back chairs and a curved-back sofa, gilded round frames with mirrors and black-and-white photos of residents from an earlier century. A soft spring breeze flowed through open windows, stroking the filmy white curtains at the windows, its caress reaching her in the polished entryway. The air was laced with the faint, sweet aroma of something baking, muffins or cookies.

Hardwood floors, which she loved, extended everywhere, emitting a floral aroma of polish. Marissa felt at home already. Unfortunately, her appreciation for her surroundings triggered an acute reminder of the disaster at her house. Clive had been willing to rush over and assess the damage. He had urged her to leave for Wilmington sooner than planned.

He'd looked up at the ceiling and let out a whistle. For a full minute he'd stared at the hole before saying, "It's gonna be a mess." His words hit her like a blunt instrument. "You might need to extend your stay down there for a few more days. I'll pull up the sub-flooring in the bathroom and let you know how bad it is."

He hadn't called her yet, so the prospect of more bad news hovered in the back of her mind as she wondered what it would cost and how long it would take to fix it. He'd been willing to rearrange his schedule to start the weekend following their conversation. She was grateful to him, and made her Wilmington reservation for the same time.

Marissa sighed and determined to not brood about her home, but rather, enjoy where she was, walking down a hallway that placed her backward in history. The metal key fob was heavy and cool in her hand.

Her room displayed a similar style as the rest of the establishment, with floral print cornices topping each window, dark molding at the ceiling, and wood flooring. Across the queen bed was an off-white candlewick bedspread.

She put her few outfits into a wooden armoire and small dresser, pausing to change into a white, short-sleeve blouse to meet the higher temperatures predicted that day. What to do first? She'd booked a few historical tours beginning the following day, but at that moment, she'd start by exploring the town. And coffee would be nice. Everything was walkable, since she was in the historic center of Wilmington. She'd get a quick lay of the land then find a coffee shop. Before her spirits sagged. Before she wondered what on earth she was doing in an expensive bed and breakfast while her house fell apart and she had a writer's block.

Marissa walked along Front Street and turned down Market Street. She walked the shady sidewalks until she ended up at the Riverwalk. There, she blended in with a flow of tourists. Shops and restaurants lined one side of the wooden-planked walkway that hemmed in the Cape Fear River. River boats waited on the other side of the walkway for their appointed tours.

After a brief stroll and scan of the riverfront, she returned the way she came until she reached Front Street again. By the time she pushed the glass door of the coffee shop, she was perspiring. She'd rethink that hot coffee and make it an iced latte instead.

The shop was inviting, cozy. A small leather couch facing two armchairs filled a cove by a window. She'd love to sit in one of those armchairs and watch the city through the plate glass window and plan her strategy for the next few days. A large golden retriever lounged at the feet of his mistress, a college-age girl staring into her phone. The dog gave Marissa a drowsy glance.

Marissa turned to get in line as a dark-haired man walked in her direction toward the door. He carried a drink and a notebook, but his head was turned toward a woman who was also angling to get in line. A second later he collided with Marissa and the hot liquid from his cup splashed across her torso. She drew in a sharp breath at the shock of heat. Her arms shot out as she looked down at her white summer blouse, now bearing a large, brown stain.

"Oh, no!" She looked back at the man, who appeared horrified.

"Oh, I'm so sorry!" To his credit, the man seemed flustered. "Are you alright?"

"If you'd pay attention to where you're walking—" she blustered and pulled the fabric away from her skin. It cooled quickly but would be uncomfortable. And unsightly.

"I am *truly* sorry. Can I buy your coffee? Please? It would make me feel better." His brown eyes pleaded with her.

She stared at him and pinched her lips into a grimace. "No, no, that won't be necessary." Suddenly, she didn't want coffee. She didn't want to stay in the noisy, crowded coffee shop. Marissa spun around and left the shop. Once outside, she wondered how to get back to her hotel. "Oh, yes. I remember." She kept up a brisk pace until she found it, still annoyed about the stain. If only the man hadn't been eyeing that woman instead of paying attention as he carried his very full cup of hot coffee, he'd have avoided the whole thing. She'd be sitting peacefully in the coffee shop enjoying her latte instead of heading back to the hotel to change clothes.

Marissa pulled on a fresh cotton top and put her stained blouse in the sink to soak. A cloud of sadness settled over her. She sat on the bed and stared toward the window, now shut. Here she was in Wilmington, alone in a lovely hotel, desperate to scratch out a book idea from the historical vestiges of the town.

Her last research trip had been quite different. She and Robert had flown to London. The first few days, they took time to be tourists, but also visited museums and took history tours. Robert had always been an enthusiastic research partner who hadn't minded pouring over volumes of historical books and documents with her.

Part of their trip had taken them outside London where they'd been able to visit modest manor homes where Joanna might have grown up, since her father had been a teacher. That gave Marissa a mental picture of what could be Joanna's lifestyle. Later, she and Robert had driven up to the Cotswold's where they stayed in a picturesque cottage with a slate roof. They'd laughed often in those days as Robert tried to master driving on the left side of the road. It's a wonder they'd made it back alive.

Back then, she'd felt *more* alive than ever. Now, she felt like a faded version of that woman from the past. Her passion for life, her energy, her vision for the future—all of it had somehow seeped away when Robert left her life.

Now she was here alone in Wilmington researching a book without him. "It's not right, Robert." Her voice filled the silent room. "You should be here with me. You've always been beside me as I worked on books." Her voice drifted into a whisper. "Now you're not."

She sighed and swung her legs from the bed. Stood up. May as well go and get dinner. A lonely, solitary dinner. Eating at a restaurant alone was when she missed Robert the most. They'd eaten out quite often, until his tumor forced them to stay home. Sitting alone at a table while surrounded with couples and groups not only reminded her of him, but made her feel doubly alone.

"Hmm. Self-pity doesn't suit you at all. Shake it off, now, Marissa. You've only just started, so give it a measure of time."

Despite her gloom, a chuckle escaped her throat at Joanna's voice in her head. Listening to Joanna's voice would be seen as eccentric. Or wacky. Of course, she'd never tell anyone. The well-known voice in her ear soothed and reassured her. Joanna was right. It was too early to get discouraged. Robert would likely say the same thing if he were there.

☙   ☙   ☙

She'd been the spitting image of Rachel. Jarrod leaned over absently and scratched the golden retriever's head, still seeing the woman in his mind's eye. Fortunately, the woman who resembled his late wife had gotten her coffee and left the shop. If she'd decided to sit at one of the small tables for a while, she'd have been a source of distraction and sadness for him.

After spilling his coffee on that other poor woman, he returned to get another coffee and settled into an armchair opposite a window in a cozy cove of the shop. He wasn't usually clumsy, but he'd had a moment of shock. Right after Rachel died, he saw her twin on a regular basis, or thought he did.

The other woman had certainly looked surprised when the hot liquid hit her blouse. Her blue eyes went round as did her mouth, until she gathered enough dignity at least to chastise him. He laughed quietly. Not funny, really, but her classy appearance and bearing were completely undone by the brown stain. When she apparently changed her mind about getting a drink and fled the café, he was saddened. He would have liked to make it up to her.

An older man sat on the worn leather armchair across from him. Jarrod nodded and smiled at him. Reminded him of his dad. In fact, the man wore a baseball cap similar to the one his dad always wore. He might think this café was full of ghosts, but his dad was very much alive. And still holding a grudge against Jarrod four years after Seth's death.

40

Jarrod leaned back and shook off the encroaching sadness. He'd come for a happy reason. At least, he hoped so. He'd called Bethany to let her know he'd arrived, but she must be at work. He'd left a message and the name of his hotel. She likely wouldn't be available until the next day. She seemed only vaguely glad he was there, which hurt more than a little. But she was twenty. She had friends, a job, a busy routine prior to his visit. He'd keep that in mind, but hoped she'd missed him, too.

Before she'd left for college, they'd had a sort of complicity. True, it had begun to fade a little in her teen years, when it was less cool to get along with one's parents. But she and Rachel were so much alike, they sometimes bickered and misunderstood each other. His relationship with Bethany was simpler and she'd often sought him out after verbally sparring with her mother.

Bethany had some time yet to finish growing into an adult woman with her own bearings in the world. Maybe then their relationship would approach a new level, not so much father and daughter, but friends. He'd settle for whatever she was ready to give him now.

A desolate wave assailed him, falling like a blanket. He pulled his breath from a deep cavern inside. After losing Seth, Rachel, and Dad, Bethany was all he had left of his family.

Chapter Five

The next day Marissa gathered her notebook, pens, lip balm, and sunscreen and put everything into her shoulder bag. She locked her bedroom door and the metallic click echoed down the empty hallway.

She'd had an impressive and ample breakfast downstairs in the homey dining room along with two other guests, who'd kept to themselves during the meal. That was fine with her. She enjoyed every bite of biscuits with homemade jam and a mouth-watering breakfast casserole and a side of fresh fruit. The meal was much heavier than her usual green smoothie and fiber cereal, but she was on vacation. And someone else was cooking breakfast for her.

Marissa was comfortably full and more optimistic than the day before as she headed to the meeting place for her morning tour. She had booked a general history tour for that day and a historic home tour for the following day. There was also a decent library and a community college library near her hotel, so she'd have several research options.

As she approached the meeting place for the tour at the intersection near a large home, she saw several people already gathered, their colorful clothing a bright banner against the lush green foliage and cloudless blue sky. She joined the gathering and stood between two couples. A woman who seemed to be the tour director looked at her and smiled. "Hello, welcome. What is your name, please?"

"Marissa Thompson."

The woman wrote something on her clipboard and asked the same question to two other newcomers. They waited another five minutes and a man jogged up to the group, breathless. "So sorry I'm late," he said, panting from his efforts. Marissa turned. It was the same man who had spilled coffee on her the day before. Just her luck. She inched away from him. Just in case.

Unfortunately, he looked at her as she slunk back and his face pinkened. He'd recognized her from their collision the day before. She gave a tight-lipped smile and a slight nod then turned her face away, hoping she appeared intent on listening to the guide.

The woman began addressing the group, panning a friendly gaze across their faces. "I think we're all here now, so we'll start our tour. I wish everyone a warm welcome and hope you enjoy our time together. My name is Jennifer and I'm a native of Wilmington. I'll give you some early background of the town and then we'll be able to walk around and see some of the historic buildings and places."

About ten people huddled toward Jennifer as she began recounting the early days of Wilmington. "This area was first settled by the English in the early 1700s, although an Italian explorer first stood here two centuries before *that*. The settlers named the new colony New Carthage. Not a very pretty name, I know, but wait. It changed several more times before becoming Wilmington, after Spencer Compton, the earl of Wilmington in England. Most of the first settlers here were from England."

She went on to describe Wilmington's establishment as a town and its growth and importance. "Wilmington was once the largest town in North Carolina. It had not one, but two railroads running through it. In those days, that meant progress, connection to other important cities, and mobility."

The group strolled along the sidewalk, seeming spellbound by the trail of history they heard. Marissa, too, felt sparks of interest, then excitement. She was an English historian of sorts, but if history was in her heart, any country's history had the capacity to stir the embers of her mind and creativity. She would count on that fact and anticipate the return of her muse.

The thread of history continued as Jennifer spoke of the Wilmington residents' resistance to various laws and taxes levied by the English. They protested laws involving tariffs on sugar and stamps.

While Jennifer talked, Marissa pointedly ignored the man from the coffee shop. With a sideways glance she observed him moving closer to her. She didn't want to miss a word but was distracted at the same time. He probably wanted to apologize again. Might want to buy her coffee. She'd been annoyed yesterday, but was over it now. She'd be gracious, but keep her distance. But if he approached her, she couldn't very well scoot away from him without looking ridiculous to everyone, including him. He was probably perfectly safe and had no beverages in his hands. She almost heard Joanna laughing in ladylike mocking at her excessive caution.

The small crowd shuffled along the sidewalks, some of which were made of brick and had dates and names carved into them. As the city's history unfolded during the tour, Marissa felt the bubble of excitement continue to percolate inside her. It had been a good decision to come to Wilmington. So many interesting events happened here, events that could easily be woven into a novel. As Jennifer described the events of the Civil War, Marissa knew that her earlier interest was getting a foothold. That was the period she'd write about. And this was the town.

"Does anyone have any questions at this point?" Jennifer's gaze roved across the horizon of her listeners.

Marissa lifted two fingers into the air. "Were there any important female figures who contributed during the Civil War?"

Jennifer's face lit up and she nodded. "Oh, yes. Women were behind the scenes helping with the war effort, as they have been during other wars. Many were involved nursing the sick when the yellow fever outbreak killed fifteen percent of the population within one month."

Those in the group murmured at the grim statistic and shook their heads. "One notable woman," Jennifer continued, "was a spy by the name of Rose Greenhow. If you'd have met her, you'd think she was a widowed society lady minding her own business going to parties and fund-raisers. Unfortunately, after several years of service as a Confederate spy, she drowned on her way back from England, trying to escape a Union gunboat. She had traveled by blockade runner, which I'll tell you more about in a moment."

A murmured comment felt far too close to her ear. "She drowned because she had gold in her pockets. Took her straight to the bottom."

Marissa turned her head, her mouth open in surprise. It was him, the coffee man, his eyes on hers. Now that he stood closer, she saw his eyes were not brown, but hazel. He was likely in his early fifties or younger, with a bit of white streaked through his dark hair.

Her neck felt warm. Why was he standing so close to her? She hoped her face wasn't turning pink. "How interesting," she managed in a whisper. "Her money or her life . . . I guess she made the wrong choice."

He shrugged. "Hard-earned cash from writing and selling her memoir. The English loved it. But she couldn't enjoy her fame. Or her young daughter or fiancé."

"Hmm. What a shame." Marissa felt strangely touched by the plight of Mrs. Greenhow. "She sounds courageous. And interesting." Maybe *that* was her prototype for a strong female character. A spy? Maybe.

She fished her notebook out of her bag and jotted the woman's name in it. She placed a question mark beside it. Then she scribbled, *drowned in 1864 after returning from England in a blockade runner. Blockade runner? Research this.*

"You're a history buff?" Again, the man.

"Something like that." He was being far too friendly, so she wouldn't offer any details. And sometimes when she told someone she was a novelist, they began gushing that they'd always wanted to write a book, or asking her what she'd written. She wasn't a famous, best-selling novelist whose books were in every airport and supermarket. She was more of a moderate success within a narrow genre. She would never be mobbed for an autograph. But saying nothing was just easier.

"Shhh," hissed one of the tour members.

Marissa exchanged glances with the man, who was chuckling quietly. "Oops," she murmured, returning a small smile.

He grinned and she noticed his white teeth and dimples. He was attractive, distinguished-looking. Why he hadn't struck her that way from the start was due to her predicament—being splashed with hot coffee—and the fact that he was an absolute stranger. Yesterday, he'd been a faceless man she'd never have thought of again. Today he was—well, she couldn't deny he was appealing, and he seemed familiar. Not like someone she'd met before, but someone who was talking to her like a friend. No formality, no pretense. Comfortable. It was a small thing, this interaction between two strangers, but it warmed a bruised and empty place inside her.

Then she remembered why he'd spilled coffee on her. A chilly wave flowed over her previous warmth. He'd been eyeballing a woman in the coffee shop. And he was being friendly now with *her*. Likely, he was one of those men who tried to pick up women wherever he went. And she wasn't going to be his next target.

She kept her eyes forward on Jennifer as much as she could during her explanation of the importance of the blockade runners, steam ships that slipped past Union blockades. They brought supplies from England and the West Indies in exchange for cotton.

Marissa took more notes, which she'd sift through later. Jennifer continued describing the remainder of the Civil War and into the late 19th century. Finally, the tour ended. There was a polite applause and the knot of tour members began to disperse. Marissa suspected the man might seize an opportunity to ask her to coffee so she nodded toward him with a cordial smile, not overly warm, and slipped from the crowd toward the riverfront.

A few moments later she regretted her impulsive decision. It might have been nice to have some company for a change. How much harm could come from having coffee with him? He seemed pleasant enough, as well as knowledgeable about history. Too late. Marissa resigned herself to another lonely lunch somewhere, to feeling like a pitiful pariah. What a waste of good food.

ℭ ℭ ℭ

Jarrod shifted in his booth seat and scanned the street outside the Middle Eastern sandwich shop hoping to see Bethany. She was running a few minutes late and had to leave about an hour later for her shift at the restaurant. If she didn't get there soon, they wouldn't have much time together.

He thought about his morning tour, which had been informative and interesting. More interesting was seeing the woman from the coffee shop there. Small world. She appeared to warm up one minute, almost smiling a time or two, then ran off like an uptight rabbit the next. There wasn't even a cup of coffee coming at her. He'd have liked to talk to her more.

The restaurant was near the campus, a no-frills kind of place with sticky plastic tables and hard benches of fake wood. The scent of fried falafel rose in the air. The place was half-filled with students and no one else Jarrod's age. He glanced over the laminated menu while his eyes darted back and forth to the front door. He made a decision from the menu, changed his mind, then changed it again. Finally, Bethany pushed through the doors and headed to his booth. She looked the same as the last time he'd seen her, her straight, brown hair pulled back in a high ponytail. She resembled her mother so much it pained him. He slid from the booth and stood, arms out. She went into his arms and they hugged. He knew he probably held on a little too long.

They slipped back into the booth. "It's so good to see you, Sweetie."

She grinned. "You too, Dad. You were easy to spot. You have more gray hair than before."

He feigned a grimace. "That's all you noticed, my gray hair? Maybe I turned gray missing my little girl."

"Oh, Dad. I'm sure *not*." She rolled her eyes, but a grin remained on her face.

No, he'd started turning gray after he lost Rachel. "How were the rest of your finals?"

"Okay. I think I did pretty good on everything except statistics. I'd rather not think about it for a couple of months."

"You're not taking summer school, are you? I don't think you mentioned that."

"I was thinking about it, but felt kind of burned out, so I'll just work instead."

Jarrod nodded then pushed the menu toward her. "You'd better decide, since we don't have a lot of time."

Bethany looked uncomfortable. "Sorry, Dad. We'll have longer next time."

He smiled at her and squeezed her hand. "I'm just happy to see you. I'm not used to going so long between visits. The house is empty without you there." *Quiet, Jarrod.* He hadn't wanted to say anything that would make her feel guilty or pressured, but it had slipped out. She was leaving the nest and he shouldn't stop her. But he wanted her to miss him at percentage of how much he missed her. And he for sure didn't want to say anything that would push her even further away. Too late for that.

"I'll come in August. I'll need a break by then before school starts up again."

"Really?" His mood lifted. He hadn't expected that, or the softened expression on her face. "That would be great."

He got up to place their orders at the counter then returned. She chatted about her classes and how much work she'd had to do toward the end, in addition to preparing for finals.

"So, what have you been doing here so far on your visit?" she asked him.

A youthful waitress came to their table with a tray covered with paper-wrapped gyro sandwiches and a side of stuffed grape leaves for Bethany. Jarrod preferred fries that evening. He didn't know if he should pray for their meal, had no idea if Bethany had continued living the way she'd been raised. He said aloud, "Thank you, Lord," for both of them and pulled his sandwich from the tray. "I took a tour today that covered the history of Wilmington. You may already be aware of how interesting the history of this city is."

She shook her head as she bit into her sandwich. "Not really. It's easy to live here and ignore the history, unless you see a statue or something. But I remember you really like history."

"Yes, I do. I still read a lot of biographies and watch history programs, so the tour fit right in. And of course, there are historic houses, streets, and everything to give a visual of what happened."

She gave him a polite smile and wiped her mouth. "Guess I missed that gene, huh?"

He laughed. "I'm sure you have a lot of other interests." He finished his sandwich and washed the last bite down with too-sweet sweetened ice tea. "Tell me about your job. What will you be doing?"

"Just waitressing. That way I can go to the beach in the morning or sleep in and be able to go to work at four or five. I work at an Italian restaurant not far from here. There are a lot of restaurants in Wilmington, as you might know. Lots of students are hired for the summer."

"I hope you get good tips. And don't eat too much pasta." Jarrod grinned at her.

"No way. I'm gluten-free. Trying to be, anyway."

Seemed like no time before Bethany had to leave. She kissed him on the cheek. "Good to see you, Dad."

"Will I see you again? I'll be here until Monday or Tuesday. Haven't decided yet." He hoped their partial hour wasn't the only time she'd reserved for him.

"Yeah, of course. I'll call you."

"Sure, okay. Hope your shift goes well tonight."

"Thanks, Dad." And she was gone.

Jarrod stared at his half-eaten French fries. In a way, Bethany had been chatty, but she'd hadn't said anything much. Her exams had gone fine. Work was fine. Everything was fine. She'd seemed evasive when he asked questions about her daily routine. He'd seen her, talked to her, but they'd said nothing of importance.

Maybe it was a first step. Maybe when she came in August, they'd have some good talks, have some fun together. She was burnt out from exams, she'd said. Maybe that was why she seemed only a fraction of the Bethany she'd been before.

Chapter Six

Clive wasn't answering his cell phone. Maybe he wasn't on the job yet or even awake. Marissa tapped her foot on the wooden floor in her hotel room and gripped the phone too tightly. She wanted to get this conversation over with and determine how deep in she was.

"Hey, Marissa." Finally, he answered in a tired voice. She heard hammering in the background. Or possibly more of her ceiling falling.

"Hi, Clive, I wanted to touch base and see how things are going over there."

"Not sure you want to know, Sis."

During their childhood, Clive had only called her "sis" when he had a scheme in his mind. She had a sense this time was even worse. She sighed. "I guess I'll need to hear the bad news sooner or later. *Bro*."

"So, the beams we saw in the bathroom floor-slash-kitchen ceiling were rotten. There was some kind of leak behind a wall that's been there for a while, apparently. We'll need to locate the source of the leak. We're replacing those beams but saw more wood that needs replacing. I'm not sure how far it goes, is the problem. There may be more."

Marissa let out a small squeal. "Oh, dear. That sounds like a lot of work. And expense." Perspiration popped out on her neck and chest. She sank down and sat on the side of the bed. From there she could see a clear, sunny day out the window, lime-green leaves peeking in, but these did little to lift her dread.

"I'm only charging you for materials at cost and a bit of labor, since I have some of my guys here. But yeah, it'll still cost you something for the damage we know about. Then, what we don't know—that's likely to be another story."

"Do you have a ballpark? I'm not sure how I'm going to pay for it."

"Hard to tell right now. So far, you're looking at a few thousand. Minimum. Sorry for the bad news. Didn't want to spoil your vacation down there."

"It's a research trip. I'm starting a new historical series and it begins in Wilmington." In her ears, her voice lacked the enthusiasm she'd had earlier when she'd decided on the Civil War theme of her new endeavor. If there was a lot more work to do on the house, she'd never be able to pay for it.

"Oh, and, Marissa—you should probably extend your trip. When were you planning to come back, Wednesday? I think you should wait at least until the weekend, maybe longer. It's not safe around here and there are tools everywhere, possibly more rotten beams. Just stay down there, do your research. I'll let you know when you can come back."

"I can't very well stay indefinitely in this expensive bed and breakfast."

"True, but at least you're comfortable. If you were here, you wouldn't be, I can promise you that."

"Thanks, Clive. Though you haven't been reassuring at all."

"It is what it is. Not sure how it got this way or why you didn't see signs before now."

Actually, she had. She'd known something was off about her bathroom floor. She'd thought it was just warping in some of the subflooring. Now she knew that floors warped for a reason and the reason shouldn't be ignored.

"Is it—salvageable?"

"Oh, sure. It'll cost you something, but it can be salvaged. Don't worry about that. Just give me a few more days and I can give you a better idea."

"Okay. Thanks, Clive. Feel free to call me if you need to."

After she hung up, she sat motionless on the side of the bed. Her house. Her and Robert's house. How would she pay for it? She *had* to write a best-seller. It was the only way out of this mess.

She trudged to the front desk where the young woman was working at the computer. Marissa smiled at her. "I think I'd like to stay a few more days, maybe until the weekend. Is that possible?"

"Let me check." The woman scanned her computer screen for a moment. "Yes, that would be fine. We have availability. You can stay in the same room if you like."

"Is it the least expensive room you have? Is there another one I could move to after Wednesday?"

The woman squeezed her lips together. "No, I'm sorry, your room is the most economical one we have." She gave Marissa an apologetic smile.

"Thank you. I'll just stay in the same one, then."

Marissa sought out the front porch, which she hadn't yet enjoyed. She sat in one of the white wicker chairs and watched a large fern sway slightly with the morning breeze. Breakfast had been wonderful, as usual, but Clive's news was causing indigestion. *Lord, what should I do? How will I pay for this?*

Another stronger breeze flowed through the wrap-around porch, caressing her where she sat and rocked. She closed her eyes, savoring the perfect temperature, the moment of balmy air pressing all around her. Was that an encouragement from God, one she needed at just that moment?

"I daresay, do *not* be worried in advance, Marissa. You are stronger than that. I simply *know* it." Joanna spoke with conviction.

"But there really *is* something to worry about. I'm in the hole at least a few thousand, Clive said." Besides that, was she really strong enough to stay optimistic? She doubted Joanna's perspective.

Tears pricked her eyes. She closed them. Why was this happening at the end of a long, dry spell in her writing? It was beating her while she was down. Was her mother right, had she taken on too much? Should she have opted for a simpler life within her limited capacity?

Or was Joanna right? Was she strong enough for this challenge, even without Robert?

Marissa swallowed. Blinked away the tears. She'd try not to think of numbers, not the low ones in her bank account nor the high ones in the bill she'd receive from Clive.

She couldn't control the condition of her house, now that she'd neglected it for several years. She didn't have that choice anymore, yet she still had a choice. She wanted to save her home. She wanted to save her career.

She had a novel to write.

ଓ   ଓ   ଓ

The automatic doors of the two-story public library opened with a whoosh and Jarrod stepped through. He found himself in a vast, airy space lined on one side with rows of books and on the other with reference desks. The library air conditioning chilled his skin.

He'd scheduled an architecture tour for the following day, but figured he could research some styles that had been prominent within the last century. The many styles he'd studied in college had faded in his memory over the years.

He approached the circulation desk and asked a white-haired woman in dark-rimmed glasses, "Good morning. Can you tell me where the architecture books are? Or at least where I can locate a catalogue?"

The woman pointed across the room. "You passed the catalogues when you came in, just over there. All of our architecture books are on the second floor on your left once you go up."

He thanked her and crossed the room to the computers. The previous evening after his hurried supper with Bethany, he'd headed back toward the center of town. There, he strolled until after sunset through the streets and along the Riverwalk, people-watching, enjoying the temperatures of early summer, and observing architectural styles. He'd seen several homes in the Italianate style that was popular in the nineteenth century in Wilmington. He liked its decorative flourish, playful "eyebrows" over the windows. Cupolas and turrets and long porches on each floor. Maybe he could incorporate some of those features into his designs.

Jarrod peered into the computer screen of the catalogue and jotted the decimal numbers of the architecture aisle on a swatch of paper. He mounted a large staircase to the second floor. As he turned toward the rows of bookshelves in the nonfiction area, he scanned the area where library patrons—mostly older adults, now that finals at the college were over—spread out their books and computers. At least there was plenty of room.

There at a table in front of him, he sighted a familiar woman, the woman from the tour and the coffee shop. She'd run off so quickly after the tour, he didn't get her name. She'd seemed afraid of him that day. He chuckled and felt a spark of relief that he had a second chance to get to know her. Or maybe it was his third. Before he could stop himself, he walked to her table.

"Hello there." He waited until she looked up and recognition registered on her face. Fortunately, no anger or suspicion. "I just wanted to say hello and tell you that I am not stalking you."

He was relieved when she gave him a genuine smile that lit up her face and eyes.

"Seems we keep running into each other," she said. "Although, this time, not physically." She said no more, as if wondering if she should ask him to sit down.

He pulled out the heavy wooden chair and sat down. "Are you on vacation, or do you live in Wilmington?" He kept his voice low, since they were in a library. At the next table an older woman frowned and glanced at them a bit too long then turned back to her book.

"I'm visiting Wilmington. I'm here to do research." Though she didn't furnish many details, she seemed far more relaxed than she had the day before. "And you?"

"I came to visit my daughter. She's a rising senior at UNC-W. Haven't seen her in a few months and she won't be home for the summer."

The woman gave him a bland smile. "That's nice. What brings you to the library?"

Jarrod leaned toward her to keep the noise level low, seeing that the nearby woman was glaring again. "My daughter isn't very available due to her work schedule, so I stay busy with tours and my own research. I'm an architect back in Asheville, so I like to research historical buildings."

"You're also a history buff, I believe."

He chuckled and held up one hand. "Guilty as charged. I've been interested in history since I was a kid. I didn't think I wanted to be a history teacher, so just kept it as a hobby all these years."

"It's a good hobby."

"Is it your hobby as well?"

"Yes, but also my vocation. I am a historical novelist. I'm researching my next series."

Her eyes caught his, as if she wanted to convince him of what she said. They were clear blue, more like a pool than an ocean, surrounded by black lashes that matched her dark, wavy hair. Her skin was pale and smooth. She seemed about his age or younger. "How interesting," he said, lifting his eyebrows, hoping she hadn't noticed how intently he looked at her just then. "What period do you write about?"

"My previous books were all set in Victorian England. I'm now focused on the American Civil War for a new series. I don't want to lock myself into just England or Europe when there are so many interesting events in U.S. history."

"Very true. I've studied the Civil War quite a lot. It *is* fascinating. A good backdrop for your novels. I think you've made a good choice."

"Glad you think so. I'm beginning to think so, myself."

Jarrod gave her a grin. "You're not sure yet? You're here doing research for your book."

The woman sighed, not in impatience, but with a deeper, more wistful emotion he couldn't guess. There must be a story behind why she was there. He could sense it.

She put down her pen and leaned on her forearms against the table top. "I've had a writer's block since—for a long time. Over a year. I need to produce a new novel or series soon or I may lose my— my audience."

"Writer's block. So, I guess that's a real thing, huh? How many books have you written?"

"Six. They were quite successful, especially the last three."

"There's no reason to think you can't do that again."

"I've said the same thing to myself. It was just hard to get myself going again after—well, after such a successful series."

"Were you afraid you couldn't do it again?"

She nodded. "That was a big part of it. Was I a one-hit wonder? Or six, as it were."

He paused. He understood her dilemma, but sensed she was selling herself short. He had an inexplicable desire to help her, if only he could. "By the way, my name is Jarrod." He held out his hand, feeling awkward.

She grinned and grasped it. "Marissa."

"Shhhh!" Finally, the woman at the adjacent table had had enough.

Jarrod sent her an apologetic wave and smile. "Sorry!" he mouthed. Turning back to Marissa, he whispered, "Would you like to talk more outside? Or go get coffee—which I promise not to spill?"

She laughed softly. "Sure, we can go outside and chat, but just for a few minutes. I'll leave my books here and take a break."

"Good plan."

He hadn't gotten any books, but was perfectly happy to get to know Marissa instead. He was glad she'd let her guard down enough to talk with him, even to admit her writer's block. That took courage to do with a total stranger. They took the staircase back down to the first floor, through the sliding glass doors, and out into the sunshine. They found a nearby bench and sat down.

There was a moment of awkward silence. Jarrod asked her, "Did you get the coffee stain out of your blouse? I have to ask, even though I'd love to forget the whole thing. I can buy you a new one."

Marissa laughed again and it seemed sincere, not simply cordial. It changed her whole face, lit it up with beauty and spontaneity. She shook her head. "No need. I soaked it for a while then wrung it out. I think it's fine."

"How far have you gotten in your novel plotting?"

"Not very, I'm afraid. I'm studying the history of the period, waiting until plot points jump out at me. I'd like to find a strong female who can inspire me."

"I remember you asked that question yesterday during the tour."

"Yes, and so far, I only have a spy. Of course, I can invent a character, and I plan to, but I like being inspired by a real person, if possible. That's always been a help to me."

"I can understand that. Kind of like a prototype."

"Yes, exactly. After I have my plot and character, I look for prototypes of the place she is from and where she lives her daily life. Even if the town I create is fictitious, I can see the details of a real town and go from there."

"All with the backdrop of real-world events in history. Sounds like a very successful recipe."

"I think I'm on the verge of something concrete. I'll spend a bit more time in the library, then this afternoon I am touring an historic house. I'm surprised you don't have an architecture tour lined up."

"Actually, I do. Tomorrow. I'm looking forward to that. Um— would you be interested in having dinner with me tonight? We're both here visiting, so it would be nicer than eating alone. You're very interesting to talk to, Marissa."

She paused, her lips parted. Then a small smile followed. "Thank you, Jarrod. I'm not sure I'm as interesting as you think, but it's nice of you to say so. And yes, I'd be happy to have dinner with you."

Relief coursed through him. He'd try not to look overly enthused and have her put her shell back on. "Great. Does six-thirty sound good to you? We can find a place down on the Riverwalk. I'll meet you at the courthouse steps. You know where that is?"

"Oh, yes. The courthouse is enormous. I'll see you there at six-thirty. Now must get back to my research." Marissa stood, but she was smiling.

"Good luck. See you later."

She headed back to the library. Before passing through the doors, she turned and lifted one hand in a small wave.

Chapter Seven

Marissa glanced at her watch. Almost six o'clock. She had plenty of time before meeting Jarrod. Her stomach hitched with nerves at the thought, but a thread of giddy pleasure wove in too. Then a wave of guilt. What would Robert think?

This was her first outing with any man since Robert's death. Some well-meaning friends had tried to introduce her to someone once but it had been too soon. She'd nearly cried at the dinner table then rushed home right after dessert.

For her dinner with Jarrod, she'd chosen a simple navy-blue sundress and white sandals. The cut was flattering on her, everyone always said whenever she wore it. It minimized the thickness around her waist, which had begun to develop steadily in the previous two years. She added a blue and white ceramic bead necklace and a bit of perfume.

It was only dinner with a nice man. Better than eating alone, as he'd said. It meant nothing. Wouldn't go anywhere. There was no reason to be nervous. Or hopeful.

She considered texting the girls or at least Eden to let them know she had a date, but reconsidered. Better wait to see if there would be anything worth saying.

Marissa gently closed the front door at the bed and breakfast and stepped out onto the wooden wrap-around porch. She breathed deeply of the spring scent of jasmine. The temperature was perfect for an evening by the water.

After saying goodbye to Jarrod earlier in the day, she'd had a productive research session for what remained of the morning in a special area of the library called the North Carolina Room. It housed valuable reference documents pertaining to North Carolina history and was a goldmine of facts.

Her house tour that afternoon had been intriguing and catalytic. The house could be a useful prototype residence for her character, once Marissa created her. That would depend on whether or not she was well-off. Marissa had brainstormed a few themes and possible plots. She'd sift through them later. It had been a good day, despite how it had begun with Clive. That part, she'd try to block from her mind. Just for now.

Marissa set out in the direction of the water, mixing in among groups of tourists, locals, and students. Downtown Wilmington buzzed with activity, the same as every other time she'd been there. She took her time ambling down Market Street toward the river. On a divide in the center of the street, a man in a multicolored vest and a black hat played the guitar and sang while people threw spare change into his open guitar case. People sat on benches or strolled, licking ice cream cones from Kilwin's. The sweet baked scent of waffle cones filled the air.

The river came into view, its surface glinting like a spread of jewels in the late afternoon sun. She turned the corner toward the massive federal building with a sizeable fountain in a courtyard at the top of the stairs. Jarrod leaned against a stone half-wall that bordered one side of the staircase. He saw her approach, pushed away from the wall, and waved with a grin. The gesture warmed her, as if she were a friend and not just a woman he'd met the day before. As if they had a history.

She climbed a few steps as he descended and they met in the middle of the wide, white-stoned staircase. "Have you been here long?" she asked, although she knew she wasn't late.

"I came early to enjoy the river. Sometimes I just like looking at it and watching the people who walk by." He wore a light blue polo shirt neatly tucked into belted brown pants. His dark hair was combed back and a subtle scent of cologne wafted toward her.

He met her gaze then started down the steps. When she fell into step beside him, he added, "Earlier, when I was standing closer to the river, I saw an alligator floating in the water. Thought it was a log at first."

"Really? I had no idea there were alligators in the Cape Fear River. I guess people shouldn't swim there."

"Absolutely not. But it *is* quite nice to take a sunset cruise on a tour boat. I've done that a couple of times. That's as close as you'll get to seeing them. Hopefully."

They strolled along the wooden planks of the Riverwalk, which was crowded with people waiting for the sunset cruise or browsing the shops. Several restaurants lined the walkway and overlooked the river. "I have my favorite, so if you don't mind, we'll go there. Is that okay?" He waited for her response.

"Of course. You likely know this area better than I do, since your daughter is here. I haven't been since—well, for a while." She wasn't ready to talk about Robert. She could have already mentioned him several times that day, but it was her private ache she didn't want to share with a virtual stranger. She'd already told him too much.

"Here it is." Jarrod led Marissa through an opening in the terrace railing of a seafood restaurant. "They have a lot of variety, if you don't like seafood."

"No, I love it. We're in a beach town, after all. Should be good seafood."

She was glad she'd let him choose. The hostess seated them on a patio near the end of the wharf overlooking the river. After they ordered, Marissa asked him, "Have you seen your daughter yet?"

"We had a quick supper last evening. She had to work all day today and I was busy, too. I ended up taking another tour. Architecture, of course."

Marissa nodded then sipped the cold water the waitress had brought. "That sounds useful for you. Are you close to your daughter?" She hoped she wasn't being too personal, but Jarrod had set her at ease with his relaxed manner and even his straightforward way of talking to her.

He let out a sigh and pulled a grimace. "We were very close when she was young. Even through her teen years we stayed close, especially when she was at odds with her mother."

Marissa tensed. Maybe Jarrod was married after all. Why hadn't she thought of that? She certainly wasn't going to ask. "That's nice that you're so close."

A troubled look fell like a veil over his face. "In the last couple of years, she's drifted away from me and she's almost like a stranger. I've made some efforts to reach out, so she knows I'm there for her, but it's not the same." He shrugged and his eyes lifted to Marissa's. "Ever since she lost her mother."

"Oh?" Marissa's head lifted as a familiar ache crept into her chest, along with a breath of relief. "I'm so sorry. How long ago was that?"

She saw a shadow of pain in his eyes. "About two years ago," he said. "It was hard for Bethany, my daughter, even though they bickered a lot. Of course, it was traumatic for both of us." He was silent and looked down at his hands. Then a half-smile emerged, as if he'd remembered something in the past. "The other day I thought I saw Rachel—that was my wife—in the coffee shop. Not really her, but someone who looked just like her. It startled me. That's why I spilled coffee on you."

Marissa almost laughed at her previous opinion of him, but caught herself. "Well, that's understandable, if you saw the image of your late wife." She added quietly, "I just thought you were ogling the woman."

Jarrod chuckled then and took a tone of mock seriousness. "I don't ogle."

She had to laugh, despite the tragic context of their conversation. "That's good news. Glad you aren't an ogler." She paused. "Was your wife—sick? You don't have to answer that if you don't want to."

He briefly laid a hand on her forearm. "I don't mind, Marissa. It's a normal thing to talk about. It's part of my life. She had a massive heart attack and died three days later. I never knew her to have any heart problems. She was slim, she was active. It was the biggest shock on earth to everyone who knew her." He pulled his hand away.

"I'm so sorry." Marissa shook her head. "I'm sure it was just awful, to have her part of your daily life and suddenly she's completely gone forever." Her voice softened. Her throat felt dry and she swallowed. Her insides ached for him, for the suddenness of his loss. At least she'd had a measure of time to prepare. Once Robert's tumor had been diagnosed, he lived over a year. The memory gripped her chest like a claw.

Jarrod only nodded. His jaw muscles tensed and his eyes darted out toward the water. He turned back to her. The solemn moment was broken as the waitress arrived with their meals. When she'd left, Jarrod asked Marissa, "Do you mind if I say a short prayer for us?"

She was surprised but glad and liked him even more. "Of course not."

True to his word, his prayer was short and simple, covering the essentials. Just the way she liked restaurant prayers.

"How are your shrimp?" Jarrod had recovered a cordial calmness, his face friendly and open.

"Very good." Marissa was sure she'd gain at least five pounds on this trip. But so worth it. "I especially like what they did with these green beans. I have trouble getting fresh beans to taste like anything at all."

He laughed. "Me too. I like to cook, but some things defy flavor, regardless of how you doctor them."

"That's one way to put it. Is your fish good?"

"Yes, I get the same thing every time." He reached for his glass of tea and took a deep draught. "Was the rest of your day fruitful?"

"Very. I think I'm on the verge of a breakthrough." She grinned at him and he gave her one back, lifting his glass toward her.

"That's good news. How long did you say you'd been blocked from writing a novel?"

Marissa looked at him, debating what to say. He'd been open with her. She swallowed. "I—I lost my husband a year and a half ago. After that, I went into a tailspin. I couldn't write anything. Robert, my husband, he'd been my muse. Or rather, my cheerleader. I don't know, when he was there, I knew I could do it. When he was gone, it all seemed like climbing a huge mountain."

Jarrod was nodding as she spoke, his lips pressed together. "It's so hard to get excited about anything, let alone the things that motivated you before."

"Yes, exactly. I knew I had to go on, but I didn't really want to. So, I distracted myself the best I could, with my house, my garden, all kinds of things. Except writing, of course. Then with time, the grieving wasn't constant anymore, but still came in waves, like when something I saw or did triggered a little memory of him. The waves wouldn't usually last long, but I knew I couldn't escape them. I'd brace myself, find a quiet corner to cry if I could, then somehow the intensity would ease up. Until the next time." As she spoke, her eyes filled and several tears tumbled down her cheeks. For once, it felt natural. She didn't need to hide her tears, flicking them away under the guise of scratching an itch. He understood.

She hadn't planned to say as much, but it felt good. She'd never talked to anyone about her grieving process. It wasn't as though that process had been planned. Rather, it was inescapable.

Jarrod's eyes glistened with moisture. Their eyes locked in a moment of shared sorrow then she felt his hand, large and warm, close around hers. For several seconds they didn't avert their eyes, almost as if they'd found a comfortable home there. Then a flush of heat crept up her neck and a completely different sentiment enveloped her.

She looked down and reached with her other hand for her paper napkin to swab her tears. She smiled at him then and he released her hand. "It's nice to be understood. One day it won't affect me this way. The healing comes a little at a time, but it seems like it will still take a while."

"It may take years until those waves stop coming and what's left is a deeply precious memory," he said, his eyes soft with compassion. "People say we'll be able to enter into those memories one day without them sweeping us away. I think that's true. I notice a sort of progression of healing on most days."

She nodded, smiled. "Me too. I have some close girlfriends from college who support me through pretty much everything. That's been a help, though the empty house is difficult at times." Not to mention falling apart.

"Yes, I have one of those," he said. "An empty house, not a group of girlfriends."

They laughed.

"They're such a blessing to me. We had a reunion just a week ago." Marissa warmed at the memory.

"From college? How is it you all stayed in touch since that time?"

Marissa shrugged and leaned forward on her elbows. "At first, we just wrote emails and Facebook posts, things like that. We were able to track with each other over the years. But over time, we all lost our spouses, whether through death or divorce. We started supporting each other through that and it brought us closer. Then we made a commitment to each other to gather once or twice a year for a weekend. So far, we've had two weekends. Those weekends and our contact in between have kept me going."

"That's fantastic." The tone in Jarrod's voice was genuine, perhaps laced with envy. "Sounds like a precious thing to have, this group of friends."

"Yes, it is precious. I don't think I could have gotten through losing Robert without them." Marissa looked away toward the water. Why was it so easy to tell everything to this near stranger?

Losing Robert had been like losing part of her own soul. He'd filled her empty places and they completed each other. She hadn't been able to talk to any man at that level since the day he left her life. With Jarrod, it seemed possible. Maybe.

As if Jarrod sensed her feelings of exposure, he said, "Tell me more about your last book series. I'm intrigued. I haven't met a fiction author before."

A stream of relief flowed through Marissa at the sudden change of topic, lifting the density, and replacing the sadness with an airy wave of pleasure. She was glad to have her attention steered to a new, hopeful place. "My first book was a stand-alone novel. I felt so new at it. I didn't have ideas for a series. It did fairly well, so I felt encouraged about doing a series. I did a two-book series after that. I like to have female heroines who rise above the place society put them at that time in history."

"Are series preferable?"

"Not necessarily, but publishers and readers like them for different reasons. Readers like to continue on with the same character or theme and publishers like to sell more books."

"Understandable."

"My last series had three books and that series was by far the most successful. I had a great character, Joanna, in all of them." Marissa couldn't stop a smile. "I really liked her character. I sort of infused the courage I lack into her. I feel like I know her so well. This is going to sound crazy to you, but sometimes I imagine she talks to me. She gives me a pep talk when I need it."

He laughed then. "Why not? You said she inspired you. It's not crazy if it works."

They laughed together for a moment then his gaze lingered on hers before he shifted it away. "Tell me more about Joanna. What was her story?"

Very comfortable ground. Marissa could talk about Joanna for hours, but would only summarize. She didn't want to abuse Jarrod's kind interest, since she wasn't sure if it was merely kindness or real interest. "Joanna's story takes place in Victorian England in a small town outside of London. Her father was a headmaster of a private school, so even though they didn't have much money, she had a good education. She is very bright and her father encouraged her, even though in those days, women couldn't aspire to very much, other than a respectable marriage." Marissa leaned back in her chair and rested her wrists on the table, grateful for Jarrod's interest.

"Would you like any dessert?"

"Oh, no thanks." If she wasn't careful, she'd look like a cow by the time she returned to Raleigh. She'd indulged in too much comfort food over the last year. "Joanna is very pretty, so her mother thinks that will be her ticket to a good marriage, since she's not wealthy. Good meaning secure, not necessarily happy. They didn't pursue that in those days."

"But Joanna wants more in life than just a ring on her finger, right?"

"Yes, of course. Joanna's father sees her intelligence and insight and wants more than just marriage for her. He also wants her to use her potential and encourages her to develop it. That causes some tension between her parents."

"I bet she feels caught in the middle, wanting her parents to get along and maybe wanting to please both of them."

"She wants to please her parents, wants peace at home, but she does want what they both want for her. She wants to marry a man who understands her goals and validates them, not just a man who wants a traditional wife. Traditional, she is *not*."

"I think I like this Joanna character. So, how does she go against society?"

"Joanna starts by teaching school but after a while it's not challenging enough for her. She's interested in business and in writing. She gets a job in a newspaper and writes a column.

Eventually—and all of this happens over the course of three novels—eventually she is able to buy the newspaper."

"And she marries someone who understands her?"

"Yes, of course. A non-traditional man in Victorian England."

"I can tell it's a work of fiction."

Marissa laughed. "Yes, I guess that's true. The beauty of fiction is you can make happen whatever works for your story. You can even place a modern-thinking man into nineteenth century England."

"Kind of like God. He can move things around for our good in large, sweeping ways that we can't discern, except in retrospect."

She gazed at him for a moment in silence. "Yes, I suppose that's true. It's been a little while since I've thought about that truth." Theoretically, she agreed. In her daily reality, she couldn't discern how taking Robert away had somehow been good for her. How it fit into a bigger picture of ultimate good. And she'd held God at arm's length ever since, like a wounded animal, unsure that her protector was still on her side.

She pushed the thought away. "As an author, I make things difficult for my characters so they'll learn some crucial lessons about themselves. And things always work out for them in the end. In my own life, I've seen a few things like that. In other cases, I'm still waiting."

"Me too." He fell silent and lifted his head to gaze out at the river, now dark.

Marissa followed his eyes. The river reflected the lights from the shops and restaurants like a jeweled crown on the darkened water. Hushed conversation and an occasional burst of laughter swirled around them from nearby tables.

He turned back at her. "Do you have a penname? Or do you use your real name, if I want to look up your books? Or perhaps stay in touch with you." He added a smile.

She knew what he was asking and she felt ready to open that door a few inches. "Marissa Thompson. That's my real name, no penname. And you?"

"Jarrod Lambert. I assume you have a website?" He was already fiddling with his phone. "Ah, there it is. Nice photo of you." He peered into the screen and his smile broadened. "And there is our friend Joanna splashed on the covers of three books."

A giddy wave of pleasure washed over her as she watched him scroll through her creative work. It made her feel legitimate for the first time in over a year. For some reason, his interest and opinion counted for her.

He put his phone away. "If I can be of any help in your new series, I'd like to. I know a bit about the Civil War. I can brainstorm with you, if you like."

She smiled. "I'd like that. Thank you, Jarrod. It's always been useful for me to bounce ideas off someone who enjoys doing that."

"Should we meet again at the library tomorrow? Say, ten o'clock?"

"Yes, I'll be there."

They lingered a while longer as if unwilling to leave. After they parted company with a promise to meet the following day, Marissa found herself smiling all the way back to her hotel. Then she texted Eden.

Chapter Eight

A high-pitched ring pierced through Jarrod's wooly cloudbank of sleep. His thoughts slowly pushed through until he realized his phone was ringing. Morning had come too abruptly.

He reached toward the phone but noticed the clock on the bedside table of his hotel room read six-thirty in the morning. The phone screen read, "Bethany." His mouth went dry as he answered. "Bethany? Are you alright?"

"Dad, I'm sick." The normally confident voice of his daughter sounded weak and broken, like a young child.

He sat upright and his grogginess melted away. He swung his feet to the floor. "What's wrong, Bethany? Where are you?" His heart pounded, yet he was relieved it hadn't been a car accident.

"I'm in the hospital. I got bad stomach cramps late last night. Not sure what time it was. My friend brought me here."

"I'll be right there. Did the doctors say what they think it is?"

"We went to the emergency room and they kept me for observation. They thought it was appendicitis. Now they're thinking it's not, but they don't know what it is."

"Did it come on suddenly?"

"Sort of, maybe an hour after I ate."

Might be food related. That didn't sound too serious, but it was too early to be relieved. Jarrod uttered a silent prayer. "I'm on my way, Sweetie."

The roads were starting to come to life with the occasional headlights piercing the murky veil of dawn as he drove to the hospital, following the mechanical voice of the GPS. The ride on the elevator to the fourth floor of the hospital seemed longer than normal, and the hallways extended forever until he found her room. Why hadn't they been able to diagnose her quickly, if it were only a food-related disturbance, like food poisoning or a severe gas attack? He shook his head and tightened his fist as he scanned the numbers posted beside each doorway.

He looked into one room where he thought Bethany was but another woman was curled up in the bed. Jarrod circled back to the nurse's station. "I'm here to see Bethany Lambert. I was told she was under observation but I'm not sure where to find her room."

A bored-looking nurse with bright red hair looked up from her computer. "Lambert. Hmm. I see she's been moved to room four-twenty-three. It's there around the corner but there's a nurse with her. Sit over there and she should be finished in a few minutes."

Jarrod found the small waiting area that the nurse indicated where three people already waited. He sat but was unable to relax. A couple talked in hushed tones and a young man with a stubby ponytail sat with his tattoo-covered arms crossed in front of him. He lifted his eyes to Jarrod then looked away. He slouched in the chair as if he wanted to nap, but was likely there, like Jarrod, waiting on news about a loved one.

Another private prayer tamped down Jarrod's rising anxiety. What was taking so long? Could he talk with a doctor at some point? He felt helpless to even go to Bethany's bedside, let alone help her with her problem She'd been fine night before last when they'd had a hasty dinner together.

In the past, it hadn't bothered him to visit a friend in the hospital, or to be there himself for a minor procedure. But ever since his three-day vigil next to the comatose body of his wife, it became a force field of terror for him. The antiseptic smell of cleaners, the hush of white-clad nurses, everything around him brought back the horror of those days. Days that ended with the grim face of the doctor shaking his head, saying, "I'm so sorry . . ."

It deepened the dread he faced anytime something happened to Bethany, no matter how minor. She was all he had left.

After a few minutes, he stood up and returned to the nurse's station. "Is Bethany Lambert available yet for a visit? I'm her father."

The nurse looked up at the room she'd indicated. "Looks like the door is opening. Yes, you can go in now."

Jarrod let out a long breath. "Thanks."

He slipped into the room where a nurse was just leaving. Bethany was buried in sheets, her face pale and fragile looking. Her blue eyes found Jarrod's. "Hi, Daddy. I'm glad you came." Her words emerged in barely a whisper.

He grabbed her hand in both of his and leaned over to press a kiss on her forehead. "Hello, Sweetie. I got here as fast as I could. Is there any news about your condition? I'd really like to talk with your doctor or your nurse." He should have grabbed the nurse who had just left, but had been so anxious to see Bethany, he hadn't even thought of it.

"They thought it was food poisoning at first. I did too. But the same thing happened a few days ago. This time was the worst."

He shook his head. "I can't imagine what it might be. You said appendicitis on the phone. Have they ruled that out?" He quelled the urge to pace the room, to wring his hands. To scream.

Bethany nodded. Her hair hung in strings around her white face. Her lips were deathly pale. Jarrod had never seen her this way and his panic rose like bile in his throat. It wasn't appendicitis, but what if it were something worse?

"I'd like to talk to your doctor. What's his or her name?"

"I can't remember. One of the nurses can find him for you. He's an Indian-looking guy. But I'm feeling a little better now. They gave me some—I don't know what they gave me, but it helped."

"Good. I'm glad you're feeling better. I'll stay as long as you're here. We'll find out what this is and get you better." If only he could be sure of that. "Have you been eating well? Maybe this is related to food."

"It might be. I've been eating like usual at home, but at the restaurant where I work, they let us eat either before or after our shift. So, I've been eating at the restaurant a lot. Saves me time and money when I can eat at the restaurant the days I work."

Jarrod frowned. "Honey, I know you want to be economical, but I wouldn't want you to eat poorly for that reason. It's not like you'll run out of money. I'll make sure you have everything you need." He chided himself for his mild rebuke. It wasn't the time for that. Foot in mouth again.

"Of course, Dad. I know. It's just easier sometimes. And it's pretty good food."

A wiry, dark-haired nurse walked into the room. Jarrod stood up. "Hello, I'm Bethany's father. Can you tell me anything about her condition?"

She turned to Jarrod. "Hello, Mr. Lambert. Yes, there was some suspicion of appendicitis but we ruled that out. Now we're thinking it's her gall bladder."

"Gall bladder? For a young woman Bethany's age?" Couldn't be.

The nurse nodded, her lips pressed into a tight line. "I'm afraid we're seeing younger cases of gall bladder attacks. It's not just middle-aged overweight people anymore." She went to Bethany's bed and checked a bag of fluid hanging beside it.

"And if that diagnosis is confirmed? What then?"

The nurse turned back to him. "We'll keep an eye on her, but might have to take it out. Don't worry, it's done laparoscopically and outpatient. She'd have about a week of recovery, but it's a straightforward procedure."

Jarrod nodded. A week. He might have to extend his trip. "When will you be sure?"

"We'll observe her for just a little longer and maybe send her home. We wouldn't want to do surgery unless it's necessary, of course. We'd like to see if it's a chronic condition or not. In the meantime, we'll recommend reducing fatty foods and see if that helps."

"That makes sense. Although it has happened at least twice already." Jarrod turned to Bethany. "How many times did you say this type of attack has happened?"

Bethany barely moved as she said, "A couple. Last week I felt pretty bad once. Then last night."

The nurse took Bethany's temperature and wrote on a clipboard. "Doctor Gupta is on his way. He should be here soon." She nodded to Jarrod then slipped out of the room.

Bethany's eyes shifted past his head and a small smile curved her lips. Jarrod turned to the door and saw the tattooed guy from the waiting room. He'd been waiting for Bethany?

Jarrod stepped back, feeling awkward. "Hello. I'm Bethany's father."

The guy nodded, unsmiling. "Chad." His gaze shifted to Bethany as he stepped toward her bed. "How are you doing?"

Her gaze lifted and her smile spread a little wider. "Better."

Chad reached out and touched her shoulder. Her eyes held his for a moment before she looked back at Jarrod with what appeared to be thinly disguised discomfort.

A whisper of dread threaded through Jarrod. Chad must be more than a friend. He didn't want to judge the guy by his numerous tattoos and dreadlocks or his mildly surly behavior, but it wasn't a guy he'd pictured for his daughter. She hadn't said a word. There was a time that she would have.

They stood in silence. Jarrod swallowed. "Are you a student, Chad?"

Chad seemed surprised at the question. "Uh, not anymore. I work in town."

Jarrod nodded. "It's a nice town. I always enjoy coming here." Of course, it was a lame thing to say, but anything else eluded him. If he asked Chad what he did for work, it would appear to be a father-suitor interview. He desperately hoped that Chad wasn't Bethany's suitor. But maybe he should give the guy a chance.

Jarrod was saved further awkwardness by the entrance of a tall dark man in a long white coat. "Hello, I'm Doctor Gupta. You're Bethany's father?"

"Yes, I am. The nurse said you were suspecting gallbladder problems."

"I think that is a likely diagnosis, but we can't be sure just yet. According to Bethany, this has happened one previous time, which isn't enough to be sure. We'd like to see her back in a couple of weeks when there's been more time."

Jarrod looked back at Bethany. That was logical, of course. But he didn't want Bethany to endure the same thing two or three more times before the hospital made a firm diagnosis. "Is there anything we can do to prevent another attack?"

"Just watching the fatty foods and alcohol. It's possible the gall bladder will have to be removed, but maybe not. We'll send her home today but I'd like to see her in a couple of weeks."

Dr. Gupta stood at Bethany's bedside. He asked her a few questions and examined her, then turned to Jarrod. "She can go home in about an hour. We'll check on her again and the nurse will come and release her."

Another hour and a half passed before a nurse came in to release Bethany. During that time, Jarrod struggled to make small talk with Bethany and Chad, but eventually gave up to silence. The nurse shooed Jarrod and Chad from the room while she helped Bethany get dressed to go. When they returned and the nurse left, Bethany said to Jarrod, "Dad, Chad can take me home. I'll stay home and rest, don't worry. I've already called in at work to say I can't come."

Jarrod frowned. Wasn't it his place to take Bethany home? He was her father. Better not to argue, since it seemed to be her choice. He'd been relieved of duty. He'd have to entrust Bethany's well-being to Chad. "Okay, Sweetie. If you're sure you feel okay. I'm glad you're planning to rest. You should take tomorrow off too, if you need to."

"Yeah, I'll probably need one more day."

As he left the hospital and walked through the parking deck, Jarrod felt empty and useless. Discomfort snagged his stomach. It seemed the rift with Bethany had just widened, opposite what he'd hoped for when he came to Wilmington. Now he knew at least one potential reason.

He arrived at his hotel and took a shower. The fatigue washed away, but the hollowness remained. He finished shaving when the thought of Marissa came with a jolt. Panicked, he grabbed his watch. Eleven-ten. He'd forgotten about their appointment amidst his concern for Bethany. And he didn't know how to reach her, hadn't asked where she was staying. Maybe she'd still be at the library. As he dashed out the door, he prayed she would be.

ʘ   ʘ   ʘ

Marissa tried to keep her mind on the volume of Civil War history opened in front of her but her eyes kept wandering to the wall clock. She breathed deeply of the aged, woody smell lifting off the pages, trying to calm her mind.

She'd awakened early that morning with a glimmer of hope in her chest. After her delicious breakfast, including cinnamon scones and fresh strawberries, she'd walked with a lightness in her step to the library.

Before she arrived, she'd received a jubilant reply from Eden. *Rissi, you've had your time of grieving and I think Robert would want you to move on with your life. Of course, you'll always miss him, but this sounds like a wonderful opportunity to step forward into your future! (I know it's just a dinner date, but please indulge me as I attempt to inspire you!) Give the future a chance! Sounds like a nice guy, too. Keep me posted!*

She regretted texting Eden the night before. She'd known it had been premature, but she'd wanted to share the news of her date with her closest friend. She'd appreciated Eden's words, even though her friend didn't take her own advice. Eden had been widowed nearly a decade and hadn't stepped into her own romantic future yet. Maybe Marissa would point that out to her one day. But for now, she was licking her own wounds.

Now that she reflected on the previous evening, it *had* seemed too good to be true. Even while she and Jarrod talked at the restaurant, a voice inside told her it would evaporate. She and her mother had both been surprised when Robert fell in love with her, since she wasn't lovable like other women. But Robert's love had been a fluke, for over twenty precious years. Not meant to be repeated. Ever.

But hadn't Jarrod felt it last night, this special and rare gift of sharing grief and hope? Maybe he hadn't. Maybe she'd just imagined the glint of tears in his eyes as she shared her story, his fixed concentration as he listened to her words. At that moment, he'd treated her as if she counted for him. She wasn't just the grouchy woman from the coffee shop. She was someone who'd caught his interest, a woman whose company he enjoyed.

Why had she not known that it was—nothing to him? Or simply not her time to meet someone new. Why had she invested herself in hoping? And why was she still sitting there wasting time looking repeatedly at the clock?

He wasn't just running late. It was too late for that. No point in expecting him to rush in with a reasonable excuse. He simply hadn't come. And they hadn't exchanged phone numbers.

She growled quietly to herself but heard a voice countering her despondency. *Keep your eyes on your goal, Marissa. Don't get distracted.*

Marissa stilled. Yes, that was right. "Thanks for the reminder," she murmured to Joanna.

She opened her browser and searched online for another tour. She wouldn't just waste her day feeling sorry for herself. She reserved the first history tour she saw.

Marissa gathered her notebooks and materials and returned the large volume to its shelf. She should stay, but if it meant watching the clock and dragging her mind back to her task, she'd be better off changing scenery.

Chapter Nine

Jarrod walked through the automatic glass doors of the library, hoping he wasn't too late. If Marissa had settled in for a two-hour study session, he'd probably see her. He bounded up the stairs, but his hopes evaporated when he saw the empty table where they'd sat together the day before. He stood still for a moment, unsure if he had any options at all.

He returned to the ground floor and approached the librarian behind the circulation desk. "Hello, um—" This was going to sound stupid, but he'd risk it. "I was supposed to meet the woman who sits at a table just up on the second floor, but I was held up. I wondered if you noticed her come in this morning." Feeling ridiculous, he added, "She has dark hair, sits upstairs sometimes—"

The woman stared at him through dark-rimmed glasses. "Lots of people are here every day. I can't be sure who you are talking about."

She was right. An idea came to him. He pulled out his phone and searched for Marissa's website. "See this woman? That's her, the woman I'm looking for."

The woman's eyes narrowed behind her glasses. "You're not a stalker, are you?"

Jarrod stifled a laugh. "No, I'm not. We had an appointment and I was late, but don't have her number."

He thought he detected a small smile on the woman's lips, though she tried to look stern. "She came in this morning and left after about an hour. Or maybe less, I don't know. But she often comes in around ten. Hard to say, though, since she's only been coming for a couple of days."

"Thank you. I'll try again tomorrow." Hopefully he'd find her then. How else could he reach her? Didn't look like she had an email address on her author website. She'd stayed in his mind as he walked back to his hotel the previous evening. Something about her drew him, even before their hearts had joined over their shared sorrow. He wasn't the type to pursue a stranger. He'd only been single for two years, so it was hard to say what type he was. Since losing Rachel, he hadn't met someone he'd felt so at home with, could talk to so easily without explaining.

He had to find her.

ℭ　ℭ　ℭ

The tour was similar to the previous one Marissa had taken, some of the same facts and a few additional ones as well. The group was smaller as well. And Jarrod wasn't there to whisper little-known facts during the tour. Was it possible she *missed* him, a man she'd just met? Was she that lonely?

As the group neared the riverfront, the guide, Bryan, scanned the attentive faces before him. "Wilmington was a major port for blockade runners. These were steam ships whose goal it was to break through Union blockades, which tried to cut off supplies to the south. The blockade runners were quite successful, with about eighty percent getting through the blockade. They'd only attempt this on a moonless night when they'd be less likely to be seen."

Marissa raised two fingers in the air. Bryan looked expectantly in her direction. "Were any of the blockade runners women?"

84

"I guess it's possible, since we don't have records of all their names. It was a dangerous job. More than likely, women were involved on the port side of things, bidding on and reselling merchandise. Some were businesswomen and others were married to blockade runners. I guess you could call it a family business." He grinned.

"Are there other heroic women you know of, aside from Rose Greenhow?"

Bryan looked annoyed with her second interruption, probably thinking she was a feminist activist. He quickly recovered himself. "I'm not an expert on that, Ma'am, but at the end of the tour, I can give you the name of a local retired historian who has a deeper knowledge of the Civil War era in Wilmington."

"Thank you." She gave him a cordial smile and didn't speak for the rest of the tour. Afterward, she approached him, pen in hand for the name of the historian.

"The historian's name is Edward Slatterly. He lives here in town. He used to teach at a university somewhere then he retired here. He did tours for a while, but I don't think he does them anymore." Bryan was thumbing through his phone contacts as he talked. "Here is his contact." He gave Marissa the number. "I think he'll be glad to talk to you."

After the tour, Marissa felt unsure what to do next. She walked along sunlight-dappled sidewalks while she mentally hashed through possible scenes and plots. A story about blockade runners or women who did business with them? Maybe Mr. Slatterly would have some more insights or little-known facts that could serve as a catalyst.

"I don't absolutely need a real heroine to inspire my character, do I, Joanna?" Of course, Joanna would agree. Surely, there were many heroines whose names were lost in obscurity, women who'd fought for their families, for their side during a long, brutal war. During that war, they all suffered, they feared. Some women were active in the cause, others held back in terror, waiting until it was over four long years later. There was plenty of heroism on both sides to inspire a character without it being an actual person, wasn't there?

Bolstered by her own pep-talk and the confirming nod of Joanna, Marissa decided to return to the library to resume her aborted research session. She mounted the stairs to the second floor and found her usual place at one end of a broad, wooden table. She opened her laptop. Around it, she spread out her papers and books. She added details from her tour to a running list of research points on a computer document. Why were the blockade runners intriguing to her? The fact that they pushed through enemy lines like determined humanitarian aid workers to deliver much-needed supplies to the people spoke of courage and daring. These would add a compelling backdrop to her novel.

She'd been absorbed in her research for nearly an hour when she heard the scrape of a chair and a quiet, "There you are."

Marissa lifted her eyes and with a jolt, saw him. A flush of relief and pleasure flooded through her. Jarrod sat down and leaned forward on his arms, a solemn expression on his face. Even with his sad gaze and graying temples, it struck her how attractive he was. His hazel eyes held hers.

"There *you* are." She wouldn't offer a smile, even though her insides did summersaults when she saw him. And like an adolescent, she felt heat move right up her neck and into her face.

"I'm so sorry I wasn't able to come this morning. You must have thought I stood you up."

"Didn't you?" She kept her voice soft as a smile played around her lips.

"My daughter was in the hospital."

Marissa's defenses fell down and crawled under the table. "Really? What happened?" She pushed the massive history book to one side and leaned forward on her forearms.

"Seems to be a gall bladder attack. They had some trouble diagnosing her, since she's young for that kind of thing. I went over early this morning. That's why I missed our appointment. I wasn't able to call. I completely forgot to ask for your number."

"Me too. We never thought something like this would happen. But I'm glad you found me. I—I don't usually come back in the afternoon. I prefer to research in the morning."

He smiled then. "I'm glad I found you, too. I got here this morning about eleven-thirty, but you'd already left. I was going to come back tomorrow." He paused, a twinkle in his eyes. "And the next day."

She laughed softly. So, it hadn't been meaningless to him. She swallowed. "Is your daughter still in the hospital?"

"No, she was released this morning. They want to see if it's a chronic occurrence before they do surgery. Logical, but I hate to think of her suffering more attacks like that."

"Maybe she won't."

"We can only hope." He gestured toward her books. "You didn't stay very long this morning."

She wouldn't tell him she'd been hurt, frustrated when he didn't come. "I'd booked another tour for this afternoon, so I left earlier than usual. That's why I came back this afternoon." It was still the truth.

"To finish up." He nodded.

"I don't feel very finished, though." She leaned back against the straight back of the chair and sighed. "I'm just amassing information. That's all."

He leaned on one elbow against the table, a thoughtful look on his face. "Isn't that how many novelists begin a new work? A plot will probably emerge through the facts and information you are gathering."

"I know. I guess I'm impatient. I've been intrigued by blockade runners, so I wonder if I should do something with that."

He nodded and held her gaze. "It could certainly be part of your plot, even if it's not your main character who is involved. This is fiction, so you can play with it a little, right?"

She smiled. "Yes, you're right. I always like to be inspired first."

"Sounds like you already are. How can we get more information about blockade runners?"

"I've been researching this morning and it was quite a large aspect of the war in this area. These men took huge risks. A lot of them were supported by English benefactors and resources." She held up the small notepad where she'd written Mr. Slatterly's number. "I have the name of a retired historian in town. I'd like to talk to him."

"I told you yesterday that I wanted to help, if you're willing. Can I?"

"Of course, you can." She smiled at him. A gush of warmth rose up inside her as he looked at her with expectancy. "I'll give the historian a call and see if we can meet with him." She may as well call the man then, when Jarrod's encouragement made her feel like all things were possible. Marissa dialed the number she'd received from Bryan. A gruff, elderly voice answered.

"Hello, Mr. Slatterly? My name is Marissa Thompson. I'm in Wilmington researching a novel that takes place during the Civil War. A local tour guide, Bryan Wellesley, gave me your number as someone who might be able to talk to me about that period."

"I'd be glad to help, Mrs—"

"Thompson. Marissa Thompson."

"I can meet with you tomorrow morning at eleven. Does that work for you?"

Marissa gave Jarrod a wide-eyed grin. He grinned back. Mr. Slatterly gave her his address. "Yes, thank you, Mr. Slatterly. I'll be bringing a friend with me if that's alright. We'll see you tomorrow at eleven."

When she hung up, Jarrod sent her a satisfied glance and a nod. "That's good progress. He'll probably be a wealth of information." He paused. "Would you like to take a walk? It's a beautiful day today."

"Yes, I'd like to."

As they left the library together, Jarrod insisted on carrying Marissa's canvas bag with her laptop and notebooks. More points for Jarrod.

Jarrod and Marissa strolled at a peaceful shuffle down 7th to 6th Street, then down Grace Street toward the Cape Fear River. She felt comfortable and content keeping pace beside him as they walked along the historic homes and under summer foliage.

"How are things going with your daughter? I wonder if her scare at the hospital can be a means of her reaching out to you, closing the gap you're feeling."

A troubled furrow appeared between his dark brows. "I hope so. She did call me early this morning, wanting me to come over tomorrow. But there was a guy there who I think is her boyfriend. She never told me about him. Not to judge by appearance, but he wasn't the clean-cut type I'd hoped for her. He wasn't too friendly, either. I would think he would be, since I'm her father."

Marissa nodded. "Hmm. That may be one reason she's drifting. She might want to spend more time with the guy."

"Chad is his name. Or else, there is something in their relationship that she knows I wouldn't approve of, so she's distancing herself. That's what I'm afraid of."

"Could you ask her? I know it's delicate." They arrived at the riverfront. The crowds thickened as they turned left on Water Street.

"Yes, carefully. I could. I don't want to alienate her just when I'm trying to get closer to her. I'll have to act like I accept Chad. Maybe if I get to know him, I'll find out he's a good guy for her."

"Parents go through this. It's universal, I think. I had a bout of it with my son, Sean, when he was about sixteen. Enamored with the wrong girl."

He looked down at her. "I didn't know you had a son. I don't think you talked about him, or else I wasn't paying attention." His voice showed mild surprise.

"No, I meant to." She had, but their conversation had taken on a life of its own the previous evening. "He lives and works in Atlanta at an accounting firm. It's his first job out of college. We don't talk too often, though I do try. He texts me weekly to let me know he's okay, but he only indulges in longer conversations about once a month." A wave of sadness drifted by. "I wish we were closer too, like you and Bethany. But I tell myself, he has his work and his friends. In the future when he has his own family, he'll be closer. I hope."

"That's probably true for both of us." They reached the Riverwalk, finding themselves surrounded by restaurants and still more pedestrians. "They probably want us to work on our own lives."

"And just leave them alone." She finished his statement. They both laughed.

"Yeah, exactly. But Bethany's a bit young for hands-off. I'll be stopping by her apartment this evening. I told her I wanted to check on her and she was willing for me to come by. And then I'll be over again tomorrow."

"Are you going to ask her about Chad?"

Jarrod nodded, his mouth set in a grim line. "Pray for me." He turned to her. "Sorry, do you pray?"

Marissa smiled. "Yes, I do. Often in desperation, but I'm trying to more often." She was glad he'd brought it up, just like the previous evening. "I have some work to do in that department, like I told you yesterday. I think I leaned on Robert far too much for everything and got out of the habit of simple daily faith."

"Easy to do. Until the rug is pulled out and our comfortable props are no longer there. But in that case, there are growth opportunities."

She flinched with a sting of conviction. "If we choose to welcome them. Which I am sorry to say I haven't done very well since losing my husband."

She hadn't done much growing, just hiding and whining. She hadn't even committed her book project to prayer as seriously as she should have. There might have been a breakthrough by now. She'd always said it was a team effort with her and God, but it had just been words. At the end of the day, she'd tried to do it on her own.

No wonder it had been so hard.

Instead, she'd given a passing nod to her faith. Even the sting of guilt over her lack of trust faded quickly. She'd made choices by not choosing. Not taking a stand.

But she was being given another chance.

Chapter Ten

Jarrod knocked on the wooden door with peeling gray paint. Bethany's apartment complex was ordinary, but there were no clear signs of vagrancy or danger.

The door eased open. Bethany looked nearly as pale as she had in the hospital, with a slight yellow cast on her clear skin. She offered a frail smile. "Twice in one day, Dad. That's a record."

He smiled back, though he was sure concern was etched all over his face. "How are you feeling, Sweetie?"

She opened the door wide and he entered the darkened space. The blinds were closed and only one small lamp glowed from a table in the corner. "I'm better. I slept all afternoon."

"I won't stay too long." He stood waiting while she pulled out a kitchen chair for him. He glanced around the living room where he saw the couch covered by her rumpled sheets where she'd napped. "It's a nice apartment." He felt he should say something, since it was his first time visiting her there.

She shrugged. "It's alright. People come and go. My current roommates are gone for the summer or on vacation."

Jarrod sat down at the kitchen table. "One more year to go. Have you started thinking about what you'll do afterward?"

Bethany took a pitcher of ice water from the fridge and poured them both a glass. She sat down across from him. "I don't know yet. I'd kind of like to stay here for a year or two."

Because of Chad. "It's a lovely town. I can see why you'd want to stay. Could you find a job here in your field, or would you take some time off first?"

"I'm not in a big hurry. Chad—the guy you met, he's a good friend of mine. Well, I guess I'll tell you, he's my boyfriend."

Jarrod tried not to show any disappointment on his face. He simply nodded. "I wondered, of course. He seemed worried about you this morning."

"He was. We were at a movie together last night when the attack hit. I came home and went to bed early, but it didn't get better so he came in the middle of the night and took me to the hospital."

"I'm glad he was there to look out for you. You could have called me, too. If it happens again, I mean. You can call me while I'm here in town." He cleared his throat. "So, how long have you been dating Chad?"

"A couple of months. We met at a party. Don't judge him by his tattoos." She managed a weak smile that didn't reach her eyes.

He chuckled. "I won't. They're popular in Asheville in every sector of society these days. Inside a person's heart is more important. What do you like about him?"

Bethany seemed surprised by his question. She shrugged then. "He's a nice guy. He's funny and cheers me up when I need it."

He hadn't looked like the funny type when Jarrod had seen him at the hospital. Grim had seemed a better adjective. And standoffish. "Do you have similar values? That's important."

Bethany's eyes narrowed and Jarrod knew he'd said the wrong thing or at the wrong time. Silently, he berated himself.

"I think you want to know if he's a Christian. I think he is. We don't talk about it a lot. I'm not as dedicated as I used to be, but I still believe. I even go to church sometimes."

He shifted with discomfort. He hadn't planned to get on that topic just yet and her response supplied ample reason. "I'm glad, Sweetie. As long as you keep trusting God and staying close to him." He sensed, as the clock on the wall ticked, that minute by minute the discussion was drawing her further away from him. "Anyway, that's not why I came to see you. I'm worried about you. I hope you don't have any more attacks."

"You're not the only one," she muttered, then crossed her arms over her stomach. "It's better now, but that was bad."

"I don't know how much longer I'll stay in Wilmington, but I want to make sure you're okay before I leave."

Bethany rolled her eyes. "I'm fine, Dad. If it happens again, they'll operate then I'll be good to go."

"Don't you want me to be here if they operate on you?" When she didn't answer his hope slipped a little lower. "Well, while I'm here I'd love to see you whenever you have some time. And even after I go back home, don't hesitate to reach out to me. You know I'll be here as soon as I can. And I mean that."

"I know, Dad. Thanks."

Their conversation ended much like the previous one at the restaurant, leaving a hollow gnawing and discomfort behind. Wouldn't she want her father there if she were undergoing gall bladder surgery? Was he *that* irrelevant in her life now?

He had a sudden urge to talk to Marissa, to unfold the wave of despair hitting him at that moment. She'd listen with compassion and understanding. He wouldn't have to explain to her what it felt like to lose a grip on his remaining family, on his relationship with Bethany. That prospect darkened and deepened the loss he'd already sustained with Rachel. And Seth. Marissa would understand. And he wouldn't feel so alone.

There was so much Bethany wasn't saying. All he could do was try to nudge discouragement out of the pit of his stomach and pray.

 C3   C3   C3

Marissa wasn't in the mood to eat alone in a restaurant. She was spoiled by Jarrod's pleasant company. As she returned to the Beauford B & B, a takeout bag in one hand, she offered a prayer for his visit with his daughter.

She sat on a rocking chair under the swaying ferns to eat her dinner, a deli sandwich of pastrami on rye with chips. The garlic pickle spear couldn't be counted as a vegetable, so she'd have to get back on track the next day. The pungent smell of pastrami rose up from the bag as she unfolded the white butcher paper.

Eden had sent her a cheerful text of encouragement that afternoon, just when she'd needed it. *Sounds like your trip is giving you much more than you expected, in a good way! I hope the novel plotting is coming together. Of course, I know it will. I think I've found a buyer for my restaurant, which is my good news. The bad news, what in the world will I do after that? NO idea! Sydney would tell me it's an adventure. Okay, an adventure. Time will tell. You're in my thoughts! Sending hugs, Eden.*

Marissa frowned. Eden sounded thrown off balance by the potential sale of her restaurant. Life was always throwing opportunities disguised as curve balls. Or maybe it was God doing that.

She'd also had a shorter text from Sydney. *Glad you made it to Wilmington! Hope it's motivating. I'm finally done with finals and grades. Yay! Off to the beach I go!* She might be alone in

Wilmington, but she was still connected with these important women in her life. A bond she needed more than ever.

Yet it was Jarrod's words that had been floating around in her head since they parted company. When had she begun to rely less on her faith, an even more vital connection, and in God's guidance? That was an easy question to answer. During Robert's illness, she'd prayed incessantly for a miracle. After his death, her prayers all but died, too, seeming hopeless. She knew it was wrong to stop praying when the answer had been "no". She still needed Him in her life, but she hadn't had the strength or the faith. What she'd told Jarrod that day had been a truthful utterance even she hadn't realized before. She had allowed Robert's strength to replace God's in her life. When Robert died, she felt bereft and completely weak.

But she was past that now, wasn't she? She still grieved but wasn't actually mad at God anymore. She'd simply gotten out of the habit of trusting, of communicating throughout the day. Jarrod seemed to have a more active faith than she did. The sad state of her faith grazed her mind from time to time but hadn't yet pushed her to action. To change.

Guilt pricked at her. And regret. God could have been a comfort during the worst moments of her loss, if only she'd allowed Him to. And now, well, she was just apathetic. Living a lackluster, fearful life, instead of a vibrant one. Her voice emerged in an unsteady whisper. "Lord, You know where I am and where I need to go." Her eyes stung. She squeezed them shut. "Please bring me there. Please help me to hear Your voice."

She blinked away the tears. Maybe He'd led her there to Wilmington without her even knowing it. That decision could have been from Him. Perhaps He was guiding her already, even in her lukewarm state, and even Jarrod—no, she wouldn't let her thoughts go there. Not yet.

She *did* have notebook full of ideas, a few plot possibilities, a direction. She'd been in Wilmington enough days to get a start putting some of them together.

Marissa pulled a spiral-bound notebook from her canvas bag. She'd been inseparable from it since her arrival. She turned to a fresh page, clicked open her pen, and began to write. A blockade runner, the woman who loved him, the fight to save their land. Then there were secondary characters, subplots. She didn't need to give Randall a fully developed outline, only some broad strokes of the first novel. *That,* she could do. He wouldn't drop her as a client. She'd save her career.

She'd call her character Belinda. Or Grace. Didn't matter at this point. As she wrote, she felt the familiar surge of enthusiasm when she was brainstorming a new book and an idea had taken hold. Frustration had given way to flow.

Joanna's voice whispered in her ear. "Marissa Thompson Author, welcome back."

Chapter Eleven

The walkway leading to Mr. Slatterly's home was of porous brick, tinged green with moss along the edges. Jarrod scanned up and around the modest dwelling. He noted the pert dormer windows on the second floor and some of the Italianate details around the sills and on the wrap-around porch. Since his arrival in town, he'd seen several stylistic elements of nineteenth-century architecture that he was eager to incorporate in future single-family home designs.

He mounted the brick stairs with Marissa at his side. She stepped forward and knocked on the door. While they waited, they exchanged a glance and a smile. He was glad to be standing there beside her sharing her interest. It was a joint adventure. A tinge of pink colored her pale cheeks, and a peaceful smile curved her lips. A floral scent rose off her skin. He refrained from breathing deeply of it but couldn't stop his eyes from discretely wandering around her smooth, heart-shaped face. A lovely exterior for a fragile yet determined woman with a depth that continued to surprise him. He'd been drawn in. Meeting a woman was something he hadn't anticipated as he planned his routine trip to Wilmington. Nor when he spilled coffee on her.

Several seconds later they heard a shuffle of footsteps which grew louder. The door opened there stood a lanky man, probably in his eighties, with wispy white hair, a pronounced clef in his chin, and silver-rimmed glasses. "Hello, and come in. You're right on time."

Marissa extended her hand. "Hello, Mr. Slatterly. It's so nice of you to receive us today. I'm Marissa and this is Jarrod Lambert." Jarrod also shook hands with the older man, whose grip was firm.

"I'm please to meet you both. Come along, we'll go into the parlor." He led them inside and continued to chat with them over his shoulder as they followed him. "I don't talk much anymore about the War or history in this area, but I've certainly done my share. You see, for years I was a history professor at a small college in Illinois. Then I came down here. Did a little bit of tour-guiding for a few years after I retired."

He led them into a bright living room where a cocker spaniel napped in a swath of sunlight spilling down from a picture window. Jarrod saw Marissa's eyes sweep around the room. He followed her example and saw rows of framed photos on every wall. Black and white photos from historical events as well as a few color photos of people who must be family members. A faint odor of mothballs hung in the air. There didn't appear to be a Mrs. Slatterly in the vicinity. Except perhaps in photos.

"Please, sit down. Help yourself to tea there on the coffee table." Mr. Slatterly settled into a recliner where he'd apparently been sitting before their arrival, as an open book and half-full glass of tea on the end table indicated.

Jarrod thanked him as he and Marissa sat on a couch opposite him. He leaned forward and poured a glass of tea for each of them.

The older man turned his gaze onto Marissa. "You said that you are doing research for a novel. What kind of information would be helpful to you?"

She sat forward against the edge of the couch, a notebook on her lap. "I'm just at the start of my research and outlining. The book will take place in Wilmington during the Civil War. It will be a three-part series, but I'm primarily working on the first part now."

The man nodded. Alert, blue eyes behind his glasses held hers as she spoke, seeming to come alive with interest. As he'd mentioned, he didn't often have the chance to talk about his favorite passion.

Mr. Slatterly leaned forward and clasped his hands, resting them on his knees. "A very interesting time period with many key events. So many Civil War historians focus mostly on Richmond and the battles that were fought all around that city, but many people don't realize how active Wilmington was in the war effort. The city was pivotal in many ways."

Jarrod felt his own historical interest stirring and spoke up. "We know that several railroads ran through the city and took supplies to points all over the south. They made Wilmington an important city before the war, and very strategic militarily during it."

"Yes, yes. So true. Once the Federals realized it was as important or more so than Charleston or Savanah, they turned more attention to it. That's when they set up more blockades along the coast. Those blockades went on for four years."

"Please say more about the blockade runners." Marissa poised her pen over her open notebook. "I'm especially interested in them."

"Gladly. Too bad the blockade runner museum in Carolina Beach closed down, but I'll try to fill in what I can. The blockade runners were steamships that could move fast. The Union, or Federals, as they were called, set up blockades all along the coast to block supplies from getting to the South. But the runners' ships had specially designed masts and retractable smokestacks, making them not only faster, but harder to detect."

Marissa took a deep sip of tea then set the glass down. "I'm fascinated by the courage and the risks they took. They seem so heroic to me."

At that point, the man chuckled, which seemed to startle her. "Well, some were heroic, to be sure. No doubt about that. But many of them were simply greedy or perhaps too uneducated to know the dangers. And among them were some military men. Yes, it was dangerous work. For a while, many of the runners got through, the majority, in fact. But with time, the Union sent more blockades down and ended up capturing more and more of the runners."

"Oh, I didn't know that many of them were captured," Marissa said. "Did this affect the supplies getting to the people?"

Mr. Slatterly stroked his chin, his gaze wandering over their heads. "Not all the runners were helping the people or providing humanitarian aid. In fact, it was largely a commercial enterprise for many of them. It was economic. They brought goods from England or the West Indies or other islands and sold them at a huge profit, or else sent them on trains elsewhere. The people would show up at the docks to buy goods as soon as the ships got to town, but some of them were businesspeople who wanted to buy goods in order to resell them. Then the ships took cotton and tar and such back to wherever they came from."

"Did they sell goods to both sides?" Jarrod tried a sip of the tea but found it too sweet. He, too, set down his glass on the coffee table.

"No, not to the North. They were the enemy. The runners did sell their goods here then take other products back to England or the islands to sell to whoever would buy them. But they got through here with ammunition and things like that, as well as corsets, specialty food for the rich, and so on. They made a killing, that's for sure."

"So, they weren't heroes?" Marissa asked in a dull voice. Jarrod could almost see her hopes slipping. She'd invested her plot in the benevolent and courageous blockade runners.

"I wouldn't say that. Some *were* interested in helping the struggling residents. And others were businessmen or profiteers. It was a mixture. Wilmington was their home base, so they did live here some of the time. Lots of them got into trouble brawling, but they made and spent a lot of money. Opportunists and speculators came, too, along with thieves, prostitutes, and all sorts of other baggage."

"What about the hungry people of Wilmington? Did they receive help at times?"

Slatterly shrugged and pursed his lips. "Many were helped, but not as much as you'd think. Lots of the wealthier people closed up their homes and moved inland to smaller towns. They did that because of the war but also because of yellow fever in 1862. The city was decimated. Lots of people just left if they could. So, prices and crime increased after that, of course."

She sighed. "Your description paints a rather ugly picture."

"You can still use that in your book, Marissa." Jarrod prompted her, as he witnessed her falling morale. She turned her head toward him and he smiled back at her.

Later, after they bid Mr. Slatterly goodbye and thanked him for his time, Marissa and Jarrod walked back toward the river along shady streets. "You seemed disappointed when you learned the good, bad, and ugly about the blockade runners."

Marissa's shoulders slumped. "Yeah, I guess I was. I'd pictured them these heroic rescue-workers and that became a strong thread in my idea. Now I have to revise the whole idea with a different set of heroes."

"Not necessarily. Why couldn't you have a blockade runner who is more honest and compassionate than others and has an interest in helping a particular needy family, or else a group of kids. Orphan kids, maybe. Then he meets a lady, etcetera, etcetera."

She stopped walking and crossed her arms, but a grin stretched across her face. "*You* should write my novel. That's what you should do!" They laughed together and he felt lighter. "Actually, your idea isn't bad at all. Have you ever tried fiction-writing?" She stared at him as if expecting an answer.

He laughed aloud. "No, it's never crossed my mind. That's why I can help *you*. I get little ideas because I've done some reading. Well, a lot of reading over the years. But you're the author. You can do it, Marissa. You have a lot to work with, given the complexity of this war. You told me yourself that the more problems there are, the more interesting the book. Not in so many words, but that was the gist. You'll have your hands full with ideas. You could write a six-volume series and have it stretch out past the war into the Reconstruction period and into the turn of the century."

Marissa narrowed her eyes at him but she was still smiling. "If I steal your ideas, will you sue me?"

Jarrod simply grinned. He loved the playful tone in her voice. When he'd first met her, she'd seemed so serious, so traditional. So uptight. He was revising that opinion moment by moment. His gaze held hers for a long moment as he fought a sudden urge to kiss her. He glanced away and resumed walking. "I promise I won't sue you. My ideas won't be as good as yours, but they're free for the asking. And I'm a good sounding-board, too."

She fell into step beside him. "I'm so confused now. The research I found was sketchy enough to lead me to the wrong conclusion. I don't mind revising my idea, but I don't have a lot of time to create something new to present to my agent."

"You'll do it. I know you will."

She threw him a glance that looked doubtful. They walked in silence for a few moments. "How is Bethany? You had a visit with her yesterday, didn't you?"

Now it was Jarrod's turn to sigh and lose his smile. "Yes, I did. It's only been a day, so she's not out of the woods yet. She rested, but she's still weak. I don't know if I'm getting any closer to her and to breaking through her barriers. Remember the surly guy at the hospital, Chad? Bethany told me he is her boyfriend. I'm being an overprotective father, I guess, but I didn't really picture her with someone like that. When I met him at the hospital, he didn't seem to care that I'm her father. Didn't seem interested in meeting me or eager to make an impression." He chuckled. "I guess I'm old school." It felt so good to verbalize his fears and his sense of rejection to her. Marissa wouldn't think there was anything wrong with being old school.

"I take it he didn't ask for permission to date her either, right?"

Jarrod laughed. "No, he must have forgotten that step."

"Well, she's only, what, twenty or twenty-one? She's got some time to meet other people and make decisions about her future."

"I need to let her know I'm there for her but not act disapproving or clingy."

"It's not easy, but sounds like a good plan." She swatted his arm lightly with her fingertips. "We're both discouraged in our projects, but we're not giving up."

Jarrod nodded. "Right." He wouldn't give up on his daughter, but doubted if his visit would lead him further in his goal to reconnect with her. He pushed a smile back at Marissa then lifted his eyebrows. "Lunch?"

ଓ   ଓ   ଓ

Marissa dabbed her lips with her napkin and reapplied her lipstick after a filling and delicious lunch at an Italian restaurant a few blocks from the riverfront. She and Jarrod had been able to sit outside on a small patio. The mid-May breeze flowed at a comfortable temperature, mixing with the faint aroma of tomato sauce and cheese. A calm and friendly prelude to a very hot Carolina summer.

"Before I forget again to ask, would you mind if I had your phone number?" Jarrod seemed tentative, almost shy.

"Of course." She smiled at him, as warmth pooled inside her. He pulled out his phone. She recited her number while he punched it into his electronic address book, then he did the same.

So glad he'd asked. Not only could they reach one another if another emergency occurred, but even after they'd returned to their homes following the trip.

That thought brought in an unwelcome reminder of Clive and her home. What else had he discovered? She made a mental note to call him, as much as she'd like to avoid it.

Her thoughts about her brother reminded her she knew nothing about Jarrod's family, except for his late wife and daughter. "Where is your family from, Jarrod? Where did you grow up?"

A shadow crossed his face and his lips tightened. She knew she'd just stumbled onto a wound.

"I grew up in Richmond. There were just two boys, my older brother Seth and me. He—he passed away about four years ago from lung cancer."

Marissa's hand flew to her mouth. "Oh, I'm so sorry. How awful."

"Yes, it was. My dad took it really hard. He thought I should have come more often during that last year. I guess I made a lot of excuses not to. Over a five-hour drive, my business, my family, yada, yada. I didn't realize how little time my brother had."

"Sounds like it wasn't deliberate, Jarrod. You had your responsibilities. You didn't know."

He nodded, but the troubled clouds remained in his eyes. "I think partly, I was avoiding the pain of it. Neither my dad nor I reacted well. He's distanced himself from me since then. That's painful."

"Of course, it is. He's your dad." Marissa laid a hand on his arm, an ache for him throbbing inside her. "But you're his only son now."

"Yes, that's true. After that happened, I huddled into my small family. We were enough. I felt protected against the abandonment of my dad." He paused. "Then I lost Rachel."

"Did your dad come around from his anger when you lost your wife?"

"For a short time."

Marissa sat back in her chair as sadness for Jarrod settled over her. "Life can be so hard. So very hard."

Their eyes met. Jarrod forced a smile then. "Let's not get dragged down by these things. It's over. I've tried to reach out to my dad. He's just not ready, I guess. I think one day he may be."

"I hope so."

Silence followed. Jarrod lifted his eyebrows and leaned back. "What does your afternoon look like?"

She knew that another difficult conversation had closed. Her breathing returned to normal. "I really should put in a couple of hours of concentrated work. I'm afraid I have to rethink my plot."

"Don't forget, there were a lot of heroic blockade runners among the others who were profiteers. Focus on one of those." Jarrod's calm, optimistic demeanor had returned.

"But Mr. Slatterly said they didn't always help the people. The goods were sent onward by train to other places but there were real needs here."

"Make that part of your plot, then." His eyes seemed to twinkle with humor and early afternoon sun, making him incredibly handsome. A ball of heat stirred in her stomach and fanned upward.

Of course, he was right. Suddenly, she felt foolish. She'd banked too much on one small part of history. History couldn't be changed, but as a novelist she could still work within it, couldn't she? But did she have time to rewrite her idea into a new plot?

Marissa gave him a grudging smile. "I guess in the last couple of years I've lost my confidence. In the past, I wouldn't have been so easily discouraged."

Jarrod placed a hand on her arm. "You have it in you, Marissa. I haven't read your books yet, but I saw your work on your website. You're having a momentary lag in confidence, as I guess a lot of authors do, but you are able to do this." His eyes locked with hers and his smile followed.

Jarrod's pep-talk had lifted her spirits. They left the restaurant with plans to connect by phone after her work session. She made her way toward the library to continue her brainstorming and, hopefully, a complete her outline. She'd create a blockade runner who was one of the good guys. He clashes with those who are only out for profit. Then there would be a strong, determined woman—

Her phone rang. Hopefully it wasn't Clive. She wasn't ready to talk to him just yet. She glanced at the screen. Worse, Randall. What if he'd changed his mind? She found a bench and sat down. "Hello, Randall."

"Hi, Marissa. How are things coming with the new book?" He got right to the point.

"Very well. I'm actually in Wilmington right now doing research for the new series. I've been here for several days and have some strong ideas coming together." She'd exaggerated just a little and kept an upbeat lilt in her voice.

"Wonderful. Good to hear. I'm calling to give you some great news."

Hope shot through her. She could use some right then. "Really? That's good."

"I was at a conference and talked to a couple of publishers who are looking for historical fiction. Lion Press was very interested in your concept and they want me to give them the outlines for all three books by next month."

Marissa's throat went dry. "Next month? Randall, I'm just working on the first book. Isn't that short notice for three?"

"It's an opportunity, Marissa. If we wait, you'll give me your proposals in three months and I'll have to shop them to cold publishers. This is an editor who is interested right away. We can nail down a contract for the whole series. I thought you'd be pleased."

"Of course, I'm very happy that they're interested in the concept to the point of wanting proposals. I'll—" She hesitated. Clearly, it was a good opportunity and she needed to grab it. Randall was rooting for her. A three-book contract was waiting. It was what she needed, but could she work that fast, when she'd been in neutral gear for nearly two years? "I'll give them what they want. Don't worry, Randall. You can count on me. I'm back in the game."

She almost heard a sigh of relief on the phone. "Good, good. I knew you weren't out of it for long. You just needed time." He paused. "Welcome back, Marissa."

At that, she had to smile as emotion rose in her throat. Despite her wave of panic, his words touched a warm spot deep inside. He had confidence in her that she didn't have in herself. "Thank you, Randall. That's very sweet. I won't let you down."

After they hung up the weight of her task tumbled down on her shoulders. "How am I going to do three book proposals within a month when my first idea isn't even on paper?" she said aloud.

See, you should have stayed within your bounds. You shouldn't aim so high that you'll embarrass yourself. Her mother's voice echoed in her ears. It was her freshman year of high school and she'd gone out for the cheerleading squad, only because her best friend, Monica, had dared her to. She hadn't even wanted to be a cheerleader, but it would surely improve her social standing. During tryouts she'd lost her balance and fallen backward on her behind, almost hitting her head on the floor. Naturally, she didn't make the first cut. She'd never been athletic, just timid and bookish. She'd also considered student government, closer to her interests, and that, too, had failed. Being on the school newspaper had finally been a fit, but hadn't erased her mother's assessment of her abilities. Nor the memory of her voice.

Three books. One at a time with Robert's coaching, *that* she could handle. Three of them all alone with barely a solid idea for the first one?

At that moment, she realized that Joanna hadn't spoken to her in over a day. Had Joanna abandoned her, just like her fiction muse had after Robert's death?

"Joanna, are you there?" Silence. What would she have said? Joanna wasn't real, but her words had been a guidepost for a few days when Marissa had most needed one.

Jarrod's encouragement had fed her discouraged spirit a little while ago. If only he were there now. She stared at her phone, which now contained his number. She'd seen him less than an hour ago. He was a new friend, but still nearly a stranger to her. She shouldn't bother him. They'd see each other later on, probably, but she didn't want to dump her new woes on him when he'd already been so helpful.

Then there was her house. She sighed deeply. Not only did she have to come up with three book ideas in a month but they had to be best-sellers if she were to save her home. Tears pricked her eyes. It was a giant task and she had to climb the mountain all alone.

Chapter Twelve

Jarrod ambled down Princess Street toward his hotel, breathing deeply of the mild afternoon breeze. Despite the mounting fatigue from his nearly sleepless night, he wore a smile most of the way back. Marissa Thompson was turning out to be a delightful surprise, and a welcome companion during his time in the city. He hadn't been interested in anyone since Rachel's death. In addition to the increasing attraction he felt for Marissa, he liked being useful to her. Clearly, she was a talented author but mired in a season of doubt. One of his best friends was a non-fiction writer, so Jarrod knew that even established writers could experience this difficulty.

He hadn't thought to ask her where she lived. He hoped she hadn't flown here from Seattle or New York. Might be hard to maintain a friendship that way. It could be on her website. He pulled up his phone and looked at her author site, scrolling to the *About* page. She did live in North Carolina, according to her bio, though a city wasn't mentioned. Of course, for her security. But the same state was a good starting point.

That afternoon his plan was to take a much-needed nap in his hotel while giving Marissa space to create her work. Then he'd call her for a late dinner. As the hotel came into view, his phone rang. The number was unfamiliar, so it couldn't be Marissa. "Hello?"

"Mr. Lambert, this is Chad. We met the other day at the hospital."

Surprise competed with alarm. He stopped walking. "Hi, Chad. Of course, I remember you. Is everything alright?"

"Bethany had another attack this afternoon so she's in the hospital again."

"Oh, no. When did it happen? Are they going to operate?"

"We ate lunch together and she started feeling bad sometime afterward. I drove her to the hospital and they admitted her. They know what's going on, since she was just here."

"I'm on my way."

He hung up. Suddenly, the fatigue vanished and he sprang to action.

Thirty minutes later Jarrod entered Bethany's hospital room. She looked as frail as the first time he'd seen her there and her complexion was a pale yellow. She lay like a limp doll surrounded by a cloud of sheets, her eyes closed. He pushed down a wave of panic as he rushed to her side.

Just then she opened her eyes in weary slits and made a weak effort to smile. "Hi Daddy," she whispered. "At least it happened fast this time."

"Shhh. Sweetie, rest. The doctor was here a few minutes ago before I got here. Chad says they're going to operate, so this won't happen to you again. I'll stay here in town as long as you need me to." At least he was self-employed and could make his own hours. His clients would certainly understand.

"Thanks, Daddy. I'm glad you're here." Her last two words faded away but he heard them clearly. His visit to Wilmington had been divinely arranged. He had no doubt about that.

ʘ   ʘ   ʘ

Marissa's feet felt like lead as she trudged toward the library. Her discouragement weighed her down to the point of physical exhaustion. When the library came into view, she went inside, mounted the stairs, and found her usual spot. There, she sat still for a few minutes. *Please help me, Lord. I need You. I need to hear Your voice.*

Minutes passed. The weight of her task and the silence seemed to grow heavier with each passing second. Gradually, understanding began to seep into her mind. "Lord, I need to hear *Your* voice. *Yours.*" At a hazy point in the past, she'd abandoned God, in a way. She'd let Robert become her inspiration until her literary muse abandoned *her.*

What about her heartfelt prayer the day before? She'd asked God to guide her and in the face of her first challenge, she crumbled. Maybe He was saying to her, even in this, trust Him. He was giving her the possibility of a three-book contract, following a year and a half of writing nothing. Not only that, she *needed* that contract.

She'd spent her life listening to others, letting their voices mold her. Her mother molded her into a fearful, timid girl with no self-confidence, convinced she'd never be loved by a man. Robert's surprising love and encouragement had allowed her to blossom. That had been wonderful and she was thankful for it. But it had been Robert's voice, not God's, that filled her mind all those years.

Then Joanna's voice—Marissa couldn't help but smile. She'd concocted that voice in her head to replace Robert's and give herself the strength she needed. It had worked temporarily. But she needed *God's* strength. *He* was her anchor. Not a human, not a fictitious character, God Himself. He'd promised to be her guide as well as a loving Father. She needed, wanted to rediscover Him in that role. Regardless of what happened in her career or at her home. Regardless.

Quietly, she murmured, "Oh, Father, please forgive me for not being thankful. For being childish, for being a complainer, for letting my mother's voice shape my self-esteem and for letting Robert's and even Joanna's voices override yours whenever I needed comfort and stability. *You're* the one who guides my path and all my days." Her eyes roved around the nearly empty library as she prayed. A lightness slipped into her, a long thread of hope.

Marissa stood and pushed aside the wooden chair. She wanted to look up a scripture she'd relied on during her college years, when every day almost frightened her into quitting. That verse and several others had sustained her, but she hadn't read them in many years.

She located the catalogue and found where the Bibles were stored. She found the shelf where a row of Bibles in different versions and languages formed a row in front of her, along with other books on religion. The words of God Himself mixed in with words of inferior wisdom.

Marissa pulled a Bible down and carried it back to her table. She flipped through the pages and scanned the book titles. "There it is." Isaiah chapter thirty.

In a low voice, she read the words, "Though the Lord gave you adversity for food and suffering for drink, he will still be with you to teach you. You will see your teacher with your own eyes. Your own ears will hear him. Right behind you a voice will say, "this is the way you should go," whether you turn to the right or to the left." The voice of the Lord would tell her what to do. He'd empower her to pull out the creativity He'd planted into her and cultivated over the years. He'd guide her steps as she walked into her future.

Then she read further, "Then you will destroy all your silver idols." Guilt pricked her. Had she made Robert into an idol? Had he replaced God in her life? Now that Robert was gone, she saw more clearly that she'd made him her highest priority. True, he'd been the love of her life and she had been thankful every day for him. Yet, he'd also had first place in her heart.

Marissa sat still for a few moments, letting the weight of God's truth and the fact of her own failings sink in. God hadn't given up on her. He'd pursued her to Wilmington where He showed her that He wanted to be first in her life again. Because of love.

Her eyes found the passage again, this time reading in verse eighteen. "So the Lord must wait for you to come to him so he can show you his love and compassion. For the Lord is a faithful God." Tears welled up in her eyes and several spilled down her cheeks. His motivation was love, always love. Not anger, not punishment. He'd waited for her. He missed her.

And she'd missed him.

She wanted to call Jarrod and tell him about her discovery. Or maybe she should keep it in her private garden, between her heart and God, the lover of her soul. She texted instead. "Having a productive time at the library. Will tell you more later. I hope you got some rest. Talk to you soon."

She turned her thoughts to the challenge of three book proposals in a month and for once, she felt anticipation, not fear. As Jarrod had said, there was enough complexity in this war to cover many volumes. She could even make it a longer series if it succeeded, and extend to later generations.

Lord, please go before me now. Marissa spread out her notebooks and opened her laptop. She'd work first on the large legal pad she kept for "scribbles", as she called them. Those were her seed ideas and brainstorm pages. She'd incorporate her research and see what plot points those events triggered in her mind.

She worked feverishly, writing in messy columns connected by arrows and small notes to herself. The first book would start before the war and go through the war period up to the fall of Fort Fisher. The second book would pick up with the post-war reconstruction period following the capture of Wilmington and military rule. The third book would deal with the rebuilding of Wilmington as an important city, growing in population following the war. The books would follow two families and, in particular, one heroic woman. There would be plenty of room for further books in a longer series, if she and the publishers leaned that direction by the time the third book was launched.

Following two and a half productive hours, Marissa checked her phone, but there was no text response from Jarrod. Maybe he was still napping. He'd seemed tired at lunch and had told her that he'd been preoccupied by Bethany.

She glanced at her watch. It was almost five. It was strange that he hadn't responded, since they'd spoken of having dinner together. She was tempted to text again but stopped herself. They'd only known each other a few days, after all. They'd exchanged phone numbers, but she shouldn't abuse it. She'd wait for him to respond.

A thought came to her as she leaned back in her straight, wooden seat. If things went further with Jarrod, she'd be glad. But she should be careful. Very careful that she didn't let him replace Robert as her idol. Hopefully, she'd learned her lesson that day. She'd keep that close to her heart and remind herself, regardless of what happened with Jarrod. *God* was at the center of her heart, not a human, important as they sometimes were.

She stood up and walked to the window, where the spring sky still shone brightly. The phone in her pocket vibrated. Jarrod. He must have overslept. It was nearly five-thirty.

Marissa walked downstairs and toward the front door then stepped outside. "Jarrod?"

"Hi, Marissa. I'm sorry I didn't call you sooner. Bethany had another attack and they're operating now. I'm at the hospital."

She leaned against the exterior wall. "Oh, I'm so sorry, Jarrod. She should be fine but I'm sorry you have to go through that worry."

"It's okay. I'm here with Chad. She should be out of surgery very soon." Had he become friendly with Chad? She hoped so. That might help his case with Bethany.

"Will they send her home?"

"No, they'll keep her until tomorrow morning, since it's late in the day. I guess that pre-empts our plans for this evening."

Though she wasn't surprised, a wave of disappointment flowed through her. "It's okay. This is more important. Do you want me to come to the hospital?"

"No, don't bother. Thank you for asking. The doctor is coming out now, so I'll have to talk to you later."

"I'll pray for you both."

"Thanks, Marissa. I'll be in touch."

CR CR CR

Even though he couldn't see her that evening, hearing Marissa's voice brought a warm comfort he needed. He thought he'd glimpsed the surgeon's white coat, but he hadn't materialized. Jarrod turned to Chad. "Have you seen Bethany's doctor in the last few minutes? I thought she would be finished by now."

"I just saw him in the hall, so I think he's done with surgery. He hasn't come by yet."

Jarrod stood and glanced down the hall for a glimpse of Dr. Gupta. Things had likely gone fine, but he wanted to hear it from the doctor's own lips. Then he could relax. It would be nice to have some support just now. Of course, Marissa was supportive, but he'd just met her. The person he really needed, surprisingly, was his dad.

Before the thought finished grazing his mind, he had his phone in his hand. He had a good excuse to call his father. Shouldn't need an excuse, but he'd take it if one was available. The phone rang four times. He'd leave a message. "Hi, Dad. It's Jarrod. I came to Wilmington to see Bethany and while I was here, she was hospitalized. Thought you'd want to know. Nothing too serious. It's a gall bladder attack, so they're operating. Uh, hope you're doing well."

Jarrod hung up the phone and stared at it a moment. Would his dad call back? Would it heal anything?

He glanced again up one hall and down the other and paced. Where was that doctor? He ached to go see Bethany, to know that everything had gone well. To see her face.

Jarrod stopped pacing and drew in a quick breath. In the void left by his dad then Rachel, had he begun to hope too much in Bethany, needing her to be there for him as his only family? Of course, he was concerned for her at that moment. That was normal. There was natural concern and desire for a closer relationship. And then, there was inappropriate need. Had he misplaced his hope and unconsciously put too much pressure on her?

Not bothering to sit, Jarrod uttered a silent prayer. *Lord, you're my strength, not Bethany. She has her life. I want to be a part of it but can't make her my life. You are my life. And You are my family.* He closed his eyes, letting the realization sink in. Take root.

After a moment, he opened his eyes and his gaze fell on Chad, again slumped in a seat, arms crossed. He'd paced and fidgeted during the surgery, his face pinched and pale. Could be he really cared deeply for Bethany. "Are you okay, Chad? You've seemed worried today."

The young man looked up at Jarrod. "The other day was the first time I'd ever been in a hospital. Kind of scares me."

"Really?" Jarrod leaned forward. "You've never been in a hospital even to visit someone? You're lucky, man." He shook his head. He wished he could say the same thing. Maybe that was why Chad had been uncommunicative the day they met.

Chad thrust a hand through his hair. "Yeah, I guess I'm lucky. Bethany will be alright, won't she?"

"Yes, she'll be fine. It's a routine operation which they usually do outpatient. She'll recover for a week. That's what the doctor said. Then she'll have to watch her diet, which I think she already wants to do."

"I'll keep an eye on her after you leave."

Jarrod stared at Chad. "I'll stay as long as she needs me."

Chapter Thirteen

After showering, dressing, and enjoying a sumptuous stuffed French toast and country sausage breakfast, Marissa decided it was time to call Clive. She slipped outside to the porch and made herself as comfortable as possible on a white wicker chair. She perked her mind to hear an encouraging word from Joanna, but the only sound was the gentle jingle of a windchime. She didn't need Joanna's voice anymore. Reluctantly, she summoned a handful of courage, closed her eyes for a brief moment for a whispered prayer, and dialed.

"Hi, Clive. I thought I'd give you a few days to do your magic. How is everything going?" She kept her voice upbeat, trying to float above the dread that skulked below.

"Hey, Marissa. Been working like dogs but we made progress. Not done yet. Good news and bad."

Her heart lifted then dropped. She braced herself. "Good news first?"

"So, we fixed the bathroom floor and located the leak. All that got fixed. Your bathroom's in good shape, except for the repainting and cosmetic stuff you'll probably want to do. We traced the rotten wood down and found a bit more, but the rest seemed good. Could have been a lot more. Let's see . . .what else? Found some rotting walls between the two bathrooms, so we fixed those."

"That's new. You didn't mention that before. Is that part of the good news or the bad?"

"It's good that it was fixed. I guess it's bad that it needed fixing. It's also good that we found the source of the leak and fixed that. Bad that we had a lot of damage to fix, and we're not done yet. Not sure how far it goes."

Marissa sighed in exasperation. "What else? What's the bottom line? Do I have to sell it?"

"Um, you can sell it if you want to, I guess. We might not have found everything and whatever else is there you'll have to fix before you sell it, unless you find an investor who'll take it off your hands for cheap."

A whimper escaped her throat. For cheap? The house she shared with her Robert? The house she loved? Sell it for cheap like some kind of white elephant? "Is it fixable, and at what price? Clive, tell me the bottom line, please. What else do you know about and what will it cost me?"

"No need to get testy, Sis. You wanted the news, so I'm telling you. Somebody moved the chimney years ago, but it wasn't supported properly, so that gave you a foundation issue. I hope it won't be too bad to fix. Haven't gotten to that yet. The whole job, you're looking at maybe eight thousand."

She was perspiring but her heart rate kept steady. Eight thousand. She'd braced herself for more. If she got a decent advance for her series, it might help her keep her house. But what if there was more wrong with it? It was a large house and might have other issues, as Clive had implied. And if she were honest, it was a lot of house for just one person. But it had been hers and Robert's. Together. True, she saw him everywhere in their house. As for her memories, she both treasured and suffered from them. Should she be willing to let the house go?

Marissa took a deliberate breath. "Clive, do what you need to do to make the house sound. I want the urgent things done. If you see other things that are important but less urgent, please make a list. Of course, I'll have to wait on those. I'll—I'll figure something out."

After hanging up with Clive she sat still for a few moments, savoring the breeze as a balm against Clive's words. The wraparound porch where she sat had quickly become one of her favorite spots in Wilmington. She had a similar one at her home in Raleigh. For how long would it be her home?

For the last year and a half, the house had, in a way, helped her heal. But it had held her back as well. The house was inextricably woven with Robert, with her life as his wife. She needed to let him go and move forward. Did that include her house?

Of course, it was too early to tell. Clive hadn't told her to stay longer or to rush home. A big part of her would gladly stay, if only she could afford the lovely bed and breakfast. She'd also love to avoid the bald reality of her home's condition.

Her thoughts drifted to Jarrod. They'd known each other only a few days but she cringed at the idea of not seeing him anymore. He'd likely be staying in Wilmington at least a week more to take care of Bethany and might be too busy to see Marissa anyway.

She was torn in both directions, to stay in a place that distracted her, took her away from her pain and problems, gave her more time with Jarrod . . . or to go home.

CR   CR   CR

Jarrod slipped on his loafers and glanced at his watch. He had a few minutes to call Marissa before he had to leave for the hospital. He knew he wouldn't see her much that day and the thought left a hollow void in his stomach.

"Hi, Marissa. It's Jarrod."

"Good morning. Did you finally get some rest?" Her voice was light, like a caress to his burdened mind.

"Yes, surprisingly. I was making up for the night before, so I slept like a rock."

"That's good. I'm sure you needed it. Will Bethany be released today?"

"Yes. I'm going to go get her in a few minutes and take her to her apartment. I'll be staying with her most of today, until Chad comes over. Would you want to have a bite of dinner later on? Something simple?" He didn't regret being in Wilmington to help Bethany, but it saddened him to miss the hours with Marissa, especially not knowing how many they'd have before going their separate ways.

They set a five-thirty appointment at a nearby sandwich shop. At least he'd have something to look forward to while he took care of Bethany.

For most of the long hours he was at Bethany's apartment, she slept. During that time, Jarrod read and did some work he'd brought with him. When she was awake, he got her water and juice, made her lunch, and got her things she needed so she wouldn't have to get up. He was grateful for the privilege to care for her in this unexpected way. It was a special gift for him since he'd felt stripped of fatherly duties almost since the day she left for college.

Once Chad arrived, Jarrod kissed Bethany's forehead and let himself out the front door into the evening air. He breathed deeply, having missed being outside. Marissa was waiting for him when he arrived at the sandwich shop. Seeing her dark hair and pale, peaceful face in the booth lifted his mood. She looked up and her face brightened. She lifted one hand in a static wave.

He slipped into the booth. "It's good to see you. I—I missed you." He hadn't meant to tell her that, but it was the truth. Her face pinkened and she smiled at him.

"I missed you, too," she said almost shyly as her gaze flitted around avoiding his eyes. "I had a productive day, though. I hope you did." She clasped her hands on the tabletop.

"That's great. I wouldn't trade the opportunity to help Bethany, but it wasn't what I'd call an interesting or productive day."

They both laughed. Jarrod leaned forward. "But that's okay. So, please tell me about your day."

She sat back and folded her hands in her lap. "Okay. Well, the first big news is that yesterday I got a call from my agent and he's met a publisher who is interested in my whole series."

"That's wonderful news, Marissa."

Tiny lines filled the space between her brows. "The only problem is that they want outlines for all three books in the series within a month."

"Oh, that soon. How did you feel about that? It's good news, but lots of pressure in a short time period."

She nodded and her lips tightened. "You got it. I felt overwhelmed at first. But of course, I recognized the opportunity and didn't want to miss it."

"So, you rallied your creativity and forged ahead." He grinned at her. He knew she could do it.

She smiled back at him. "Well, I guess you could say that. God really helped me. It was like a special force filled me with ideas and I was able to get a lot of it done yesterday and again today. It was—" she splayed her hands, "—humbling."

Impulsively, he grabbed both of her hands in his and squeezed them. Her blue-gray eyes flew to his and her cheeks colored again.

He released her hands. Maybe he'd gone too far. "I'm so glad, Marissa. I knew you could do it."

Once she recovered her surprise, she seemed pleased rather than bothered by his gesture. Then her face clouded. "I really *need* to do it." She sighed deeply and her eyes met his. "My historic house is falling apart and I'm already in the hole over eight thousand dollars."

Jarrod let out a low whistle. "Oh, that's a pocket of change. I'm sorry to hear that. It puts more pressure on you in your need to come up with your trilogy."

"Yes, lots of it. I guess it will all come out in the wash, but I'm not exactly sure how I'll pay for it or how much more damage is there."

"I'm an architect. Can I be of help?"

"I don't know. You're not a contractor, but I guess you'd understand how things are put together. My brother, Clive, is a contractor and he's working on it at cost." She waved the air with one hand. "Anyway, you've been so helpful already, I couldn't ask you to do anymore."

He caught her gaze and held it to make sure she knew he was serious. "Marissa, if I can help, I'm willing to. I don't know if I can, but I can make a phone call to Clive, if you want."

"That's very sweet of you. I—I can mention it to Clive and see if he thinks that would be useful in this mess." She smiled but it didn't reach her eyes. "Thank you, Jarrod." Her eyes locked his for a moment then darted to the menus. "Maybe we should have a look?" She slid one of the menus across the table toward him.

Good idea. Otherwise, they'd sit there talking and never get around to eating.

He wanted to ask her how long she would be staying but didn't want to hear her response. He could likely see her a few more times before he returned to Asheville, between his shifts with Bethany. Bethany would be doing better by tomorrow.

He'd savor every moment while they had time.

Later as he walked home, his phone rang. He lifted his brows in surprise and answered. "Hi, Dad. I guess you got my message."

"Yes, I was surprised to hear about Bethany." Dad's voice sounded older, thinner than before. Jarrod thought he detected a trace of warmth in it. Might be wishful thinking.

"Gall bladder, you said? She'll be alright, won't she?"

"Yes, she should be. Normally it's an outpatient procedure, but they're keeping her overnight." He waited. There were a few seconds of silence. Then he heard his dad clear his throat.

"I'm glad you called me. Let me know how she makes out, once it's over, okay? Once she's recovered, maybe you two can come up for a weekend. And maybe plan on Christmas, too, if you don't have other plans."

Jarrod almost dropped the phone from surprise. "I'd like that, Dad. Thanks. I'll call you in a couple of days and let you know how she is."

After he hung up, he stood for a moment in the light of the pink strips of setting sun on the horizon, enjoying the feeling of hope that coursed through his veins and heart. "Thank you, Lord. May this be a beginning."

Maybe Marissa had prayed, and her prayers had been heard. Or maybe it was just time for Jarrod's Dad to realize he still had a son. And a granddaughter.

Chapter Fourteen

Day seven in Wilmington. It was time to go home.

Marissa's eyes roved around the details of the quaint dining room as she finished her breakfast, a Portobello mushroom and Swiss omelet with real bacon sprinkles on top along with honey bran muffins. In addition to likely gaining five pounds, her research trip had turned into much more than she'd expected. Spiritually, she felt renewed, with a fresh breath of God's centrality in her life. In a new way, her present and her future were back on track.

The door to her creativity had burst wide-open, giving her a clear path for all three books in her series, with a grasp of her basic story line. She still had to write them, but the hardest part, her mental attitude, was intact and on track. And she already had a publisher interested in seeing them. *That* didn't often happen so easily.

Then there was Jarrod. That brought her momentum halting at a question mark. What would become of her friendship with him? She ought to tell him she'd like to see him again, but doubted she'd have the nerve.

Her objectives had been accomplished. Any delay would be pure avoidance. If something were meant to happen with Jarrod, it would. She didn't have to stay in Wilmington for his sake. He'd be busy with Bethany for several more days, though since her surgery, he'd done his best to squeeze in a dinner or phone call when he could.

If she left that afternoon by three, she'd be back in Raleigh by dinnertime, just as rush hour began. According to Clive, her home wasn't dangerous anymore. There were still unsightly messes in several rooms, but it was livable. Being on site would give her the hands-on ability to decide what to do and when.

She would spend her last morning in Wilmington taking a final walk around the town. She'd take her time, savoring the details that might have eluded her during those first few days when she'd been anxious and lost. In the afternoon she'd spend about an hour at the museum to finish looking at the Civil War displays. She hoped Jarrod would have time to see her before she left.

Marissa sent a text message to him. "Hi Jarrod, I will need to leave Wilmington soon, unfortunately. It's been a great week." She stared at her message. No, it sounded too final. She replaced the second sentence with, "Please give me a call when you have a chance." She could tell him when he called that she'd be leaving later that day. The next move would be his.

She pulled her folded clothes from the antique dresser and placed them in her suitcase. After checking the shower and bathroom for her toiletries and anything else she'd forgotten, she zipped her suitcase shut. A final glance around the room and under the bed and she reached for the bulky metal key for the last time.

Checkout was quick and simple. Thank goodness for credit cards. By the time the bill came at the end of next month, maybe she'd have a notion of how she'd pay it.

Although she was encouraged by the week's accomplishments, melancholy hovered over her like a gray cloud as she put her suitcase and the bag containing her laptop and legal pads into the trunk of her car. Jarrod hadn't called in the last hour since she'd texted him. Maybe he hadn't read her message yet. Or else the news of her departure hadn't fazed him.

She'd be fine, she knew that. Without Robert nudging her, encouraging her, brainstorming with her. Without Joanna's perky British voice coaching or coaxing. Even without Jarrod's calm but focused attention as he expressed his belief in her. She'd begun to believe in herself. With God's voice alone, she'd find her way. She'd known it in theory but hadn't tested it. It was time for her to own it.

CR   CR   CR

At noon, Jarrod sat across from Bethany at her small dining room table, eating bowls of canned soup which he'd heated up. She'd insisted that she was well-rested and on the mend, but she already looked drowsy.

She ate her soup delicately then suddenly, glancing mischievously at Jarrod, slurped loudly like she used to do as a preteen to get a laugh. They both laughed. "Haven't done that in a while." She grinned at him. So like the old Bethany, it made his chest hurt.

"No, you haven't. I sort of missed it." Among other things. "And the burps and the bad hair days and the complaining about horrible dates."

She shook her head, a smile still curving her lips. "You don't forget anything, do you?"

"Good and bad, they're all special memories."

Her smile fell and she stared at the table. "Dad, I need to tell you something."

Jarrod tensed. Waited.

When her face lifted, her eyes were shiny with tears. She paused and licked her lips. Swallowed. Then with a deep breath, she spoke. "When Mom died, I didn't know what to do. I was, like, crazy. Like my heart had exploded. I didn't know anyone who'd been through that and, honestly, I never thought I would go through it. Mom was there, normal, then suddenly she was—gone." Her voice broke. Several tears tumbled down her cheeks.

Jarrod's eyes stung. He reached out and took Bethany's hand. He squeezed it and she squeezed back, her hand warm and moist.

"So, when I came here to school, I was far away from it. I still missed her, but it was a lot easier to be away from the house. It was like, I had so much here that was different that it made me feel better. Even living another way from how I'd been raised felt better. Like I was a different person who hadn't been through all that. I know that's terrible to say."

"No, it isn't, Sweetie." Jarrod kept his tone quiet, his eyes fixed on his daughter. "It's normal. Understandable."

She sniffed. "But here's the really bad part. You were part of *her*, so I avoided you, too. You didn't do anything wrong, but you reminded me of what I lost. But I didn't even stop to think that you'd lost her, too."

Tears flowed freely down her cheeks and her grip tightened on his. She bowed her head. A sob escaped her throat. "I'm so sorry, Dad. I'm so sorry."

She lifted her head. Her face was pink and wet, but it was the most beautiful sight he'd ever seen.

"Dad, I've missed you so much. But my heart was dying for a while. But the thing is, yours was too."

He nodded as his own tears flowed freely down his cheeks. "Yes, my heart was dying, too. We both miss your Mom. We always will, to some degree. But I understand your distance."

Jarrod rose and went to her. She stood and let him wrap his arms around her shoulders. "I've missed you, too. You've always been my Sweetie, and you always will be. My sweet girl," he whispered into her hair.

She pulled back. "Do you forgive me?"

He almost laughed. "Of course, I do. I love you, Bethany. I'll always forgive you of anything, but please always be part of my life. I couldn't bear it any other way."

Bethany nodded. "I need that, too. I want it back." She sniffed again and he handed her a napkin. She blew her nose loudly and grinned at him. Like old times.

While Bethany napped, Jarrod couldn't read, couldn't concentrate on anything but the miracle that had happened. The second one in two days. "Thank you, God. Thank you, thank you," he prayed over and over. He had his little girl back.

During the afternoon, he fell asleep, too, as peaceful contentment and drowsiness overcame him. When he awoke, it was almost three o'clock. With a start, he realized he hadn't called Marissa. She must be wondering what his plans were or why he hadn't called. There were two text messages from her. His heart sank when he read the first one, "Hi Jarrod, I will need to leave Wilmington soon, unfortunately. Please give me a call when you have a chance." It had come at ten-thirty that morning. Her second message read, "I don't know if you received my first message. I have to leave Wilmington today. I'm leaving today at around three. I hope to talk to you."

He hastened to dial her number, his fingers fumbling. It went into voicemail. Had she left already? He left a message. "Marissa? I'm sorry I didn't call earlier. I've had a breakthrough with Bethany and—I'm so sorry I didn't respond. Are you still here? I hope so. I'll be there by three. Please don't leave until I see you."

What if she didn't get the message in time? How stupid he was to let the whole day go by, thinking he had time to reach her later.

Later wouldn't come. Maybe she'd get a text more easily. "Marissa, please don't leave yet! I'll be there by three. I'm on my way."

Fortunately, Bethany was stirring on the couch where she'd been napping. "Honey, are you awake?" He stood over where she lay on the couch. Her eyes opened and she yawned. "I have to leave for a little bit. I can come back afterward."

"Okay, Dad. I'll be okay. You don't need to come back today. Chad will be here, I think. Or Nicole. She's my roommate."

"I'll see you soon, Sweetie." But she'd already fallen back to sleep.

Jarrod hurried out of the apartment and down the wooden flight of stairs. He prayed Marissa would get his message and wait for him. Then what would he say to her? He'd figure that out when he got there. He cursed himself as he slipped into his car and started the ignition. He needed to see her before she left Wilmington.

℘   ℘   ℘

Marissa looked at her watch. She should have called Jarrod instead of texting. Texts were easy to ignore or overlook. Too late now. She could always return to Raleigh and allow a week to go by then call him to inquire about Bethany. Of course, she cared about Bethany, but it would also give her an excuse to call.

For what felt like the tenth time, she checked her texts. Nothing from Jarrod, but a text from Julia. *Hi Marissa. Hope all is going well in Wilmington.* She had no idea. More than well, Julia.

Marissa smiled, but it died on her lips as she read Julia's next lines. *My mom has taken a turn for the worse, so I need prayer! She's come down with a virus or something and in her condition, that could be really bad. I spend most of my time there now and*

132

my business is on the back burner. I'm preparing for the worst. Thanks for your prayers. Julia.

Marissa's heart ached for Julia. Marissa hadn't been close to her own mother, so could only guess at the pain her friend was experiencing. Julia's mother had come over from Italy and raised her as a single mom. She silently prayed for Julia's mother and peace for her friend.

She sighed deeply and looked around her at the tranquil setting. Seemed like more than a week that she'd been there, and it had found its way inside her. She'd miss the porch and the swaying ferns over the white, wicker furniture. The establishment had given her a peaceful place to land, to sort out the details of her life. In the end, God had intervened on a daily basis. Despite the ache in her heart for Julia and for the end of her week in Wilmington, Marissa smiled.

All day long she'd put off calling Clive, not wanting to miss Jarrod's call. But finally, she had to call and let him know she was on her way. She'd left her return date hanging the last time they'd spoken. "I'll be home tonight by six, barring traffic," she'd told him.

"Okay, it won't be pretty, but it's safe. Come on home."

She should have left already but wanted to give Jarrod a few more minutes. Maybe he had texted while she was talking to Clive. She checked her phone and he'd left a text. A wave of relief rolled over her. He was on his way.

It was three twenty. Marissa felt a bit nervous, as if they were about to go on their first date. She'd become so comfortable with him, why the nerves now? Because it was her last time to see him in Wilmington. At least he hadn't said it had been nice to meet her and good luck with her books. At least he was coming to see her before she left.

She looked up as a car pulled away from the curb and drove away. Another car slid into the space. Jarrod got out and stood by the car, a panicked expression on his face. She waved. He circled the car and bounded up the steps to join her on a wicker chair. His cheeks were rosy with exertion as if he'd come on foot instead of by car.

"I'm so glad I caught you. I'm so sorry I didn't phone this morning. I guess—" he shook his head and splayed his hands. "I thought we had more time. When did you decide to leave?"

"Just this morning. I apologize for the abruptness." Her eyes caught his. She hoped he'd see how much she regretted leaving. "I'm not usually like that. Truth is, I was putting off going home. I could always justify more research, but I needed to face the damage of my house. Also, I didn't think I could afford to stay here much longer." She hitched her head toward the doorway of the bed and breakfast.

"I understand, after what you told me about your house yesterday." He paused. "Did you get my voice message about Bethany?"

She shook her head. "Is she okay?"

He grinned, long dimples appearing on his cheeks. "Very okay. She finally told me why she'd gotten distant. I reminded her of her mother, and it was too difficult for her."

Marissa swallowed. "She told you that today?"

He nodded. "It meant so much to me. I felt like I got her back today."

"That's wonderful, Jarrod. I'm so happy for you. How much longer do you think you'll need to stay here?"

"I don't know how much help she's going to need. Another day or so. One of her roommates is coming back later tonight. Then there's always Chad."

"The famous Chad." Marissa chuckled.

"Now that she and I are closer, I hope she'll tell me more about him. But one thing at a time."

"Yes. That's a good plan."

"My dad called, too. About Bethany. I'm hopeful that will heal some things, too. It's been a good week for family issues. And I think a good one for you, too. For novels."

"Yes, it has. I'm so glad about your daughter and your dad. I hope that healing continues." She smiled and waited.

Silence fell between them. Then he turned to her. "I don't want to keep you, Marissa. But—how do I say this? We've only just met but I feel like I've known you for a long time. You're different than other women I've met since being widowed. I felt comfortable with you right away. We didn't have this awkward phase. At least, I didn't have that."

"I didn't either. In spite of the coffee." They both laughed.

He sobered and his eyes found hers. Hazel eyes flecked with gold and rimmed with dark lashes. Eyes she'd never forget. "Marissa, I'd like to see you again."

"I'd like to see you, too." There, she'd said it. His confession had made it so easy. That, and the eager look on his handsome face.

"I don't even know where you live. I kept meaning to ask."

"I live in Raleigh."

"Raleigh." He nodded. "It's a bit far for a date, but we could work something out, couldn't we?"

They laughed again and a light, joyful feeling filled her chest. She couldn't possibly have returned to Raleigh without knowing if she'd see him again. "I'm sure we could. You're in Asheville, right? A four-hour drive."

He nodded. Then his eyes widened. "I just thought of something. Recently, I got a new client in Raleigh, but I delegated it to this young architect who is working for me for a few months to get some experience. I can un-delegate it and give him something else."

"There's an idea!" She clasped her hands together.

"Normally, I don't need to visit clients very much. We do everything on the phone or computer, but I could make an exception once in a while, especially in the beginning of my work with them. And of course, I'll invite you to Asheville. You could write a book that takes place there, couldn't you? A sequel?"

She had to laugh at his enthusiasm. "You're so full of ideas for my career. Let's take it one day at a time. You could call me, for example."

"That, I will do, Marissa Thompson. Probably very soon."

They looked at each other in silence for a moment, both smiling. Warmth tingled up her neck. Happiness flowed through her body until she felt saturated by it.

Jarrod stood. "May I walk you to your car? I don't want you to leave, but I think I'm holding you up."

She took his proffered hand and got to her feet. They walked down the brick steps. "No, you're not. I'm not *willing* to leave, but I have to." She stopped walking and looked up at him. "But I could possibly wait another hour or so. If I left now, I'd be arriving at rush hour. It's the worst time to arrive."

"Well, then, you shouldn't leave now. It would be wiser to wait." He gave her a grave look then a grin crept across his face.

"We could have coffee. Remember, I never let you buy me coffee that day?"

"Yes, I do remember that I owe you a coffee. May I invite you to have coffee with me?"

"Yes, you may. And I'd be happy to accept this time."

"I promise to keep the coffee in the cup. Our coffee shop is that direction." He pointed down the street then held out one arm to her.

She curled her fingers around it and together they walked down the street toward the riverfront.

I hope you enjoyed reading *Marissa Rewritten*. If you did, please consider leaving a review at the store where you purchased it. This will help other readers discover my books and be encouraged by their inspiring truths. You can also sign up to receive updates about new books (*and* read the first chapter of all my books) at www.Kyle-Hunter.com

In this book, you read that Marissa and her three friends from college have reunited, twenty-five years later, and decided to get together twice a year for a weekend reunion. Each of these women has a history of her own, along with desires, mistakes, and sometimes, secrets.

Marissa Rewritten is the first book of the series, followed by **three full-length novels**, one for each of Marissa's friends: Julia, Sydney, and Eden.

Join them in their own stories!

*After Marissa Rewritten, read **Julia Redesigned**, Book 2 in the Second Chance Series. Find out more . . .*

Julia Redesigned (*Second Chance Series: Book 2*)

Can a stack of letters provide clues to an age-old conflict and a doorway to a new family?

For the last three years, Julia De Luca has juggled her successful interior design business with caring for her elderly mother. Following her mother's death, Julia finds old letters from distant relatives in Italy. They remind her of visits she and her mother made when Julia was a child. Could these letters hold the answer to why their trips to Italy ended abruptly when she was ten years old?

These people whose names she's forgotten are the only family Julia has left on earth. How can she reconnect with them after so many years? Would it be crazy to try?

Her compelling desire to locate her distant family leads Julia on an impulsive trip to Florence, Italy. Along with savoring the sights and flavors of Florence, Julia discovers that families can be messy, that it's not too late to fall in love, and that there's more to Julia De Luca than she ever knew.

(Coming Soon: **Sydney Rewound**: Book 3)

More stories that take you places . . .

One December

Is there any way to recapture what happened under a Christmas moon one December?

Nikki has loved Mike for as long as she can remember (as early as age seven!) Mike has his own past hurts to resolve, having lost both parents in an accident when he was fourteen. He's tried to escape those painful memories by leaving New York and starting a new life on the West Coast. New facts indicate, years later, that his parents' deaths might not have been an accident.

At Christmas Mike comes back to New York for the first time in three years. He and Nikki rekindle the friendship they had as children and share their newfound faith. Under a Christmas moon romantic sparks fly . . . but their mutual attraction takes an unexpected detour.

Nikki is devastated, believing her one chance for a relationship with Mike is over. She impulsively takes a one-year teaching opportunity in Paris, so that she can face her own fears *and* get over Mike.

If Mike and Nikki run away, how can they find each other again?

"*One December* sizzles with romantic tension, taking the reader on a roller-coaster ride from New York to San Francisco, with a delightful detour in Paris. I couldn't put it down!"
– Elizabeth Musser, author of *The Secrets of the Cross* trilogy and *The Swan House.*

Circle Back Around

Hailey and her father haven't always seen eye to eye, especially in running the failing family textile mill. Frustrated, Hailey leaves the mill and her hometown in North Carolina to start a new life near her sister in Colorado. Only months later her father calls to ask a special favor. He needs heart surgery and asks Hailey to run the mill in his place.

Moving back would devastate Hailey's sister, Hope. Yet Hailey would have an opportunity to possibly save the mill, and at a time when her father needs her most. And maybe he'd even approve of her for the first time in her life.

Filled with self-doubt, Hailey returns to North Carolina and struggles to make a difference at the mill, facing more challenges than she bargained for. Her attractive neighbor, Alex, is almost enough to outweigh the difficulties, but she doesn't know that in the shadows lurks someone who wants to destroy both her *and* the mill.

Prodigals in Provence *(Book 1: The Provence Series)*

Bree and Lauren own and run Le Bon Voyage, a travel company specializing in tours to charming Provence, France.

Travis is a TV travel critic accustomed to crossing the globe to film documentaries and write books. But he's been in a spiritual desert ever since losing his marriage and ministry five years earlier.

Between film projects, Travis plans to accompany his elderly mother on a tour to Provence, a long-term dream for her. Bree tries unsuccessfully to block him, sure he's coming to spy on the struggling company for one of his exposé articles.

A diverse group of tourists arrives at the rented villa to spend the week and discover the spectacular villages, vineyards, and history of the Luberon mountain region of Provence. Amidst a series of problems and relational tensions, Bree thinks she has all she can handle . . . until she becomes attracted to Travis.

As Bree and Travis are drawn together, will their hidden wounds drive them apart?

A Promise in Provence *(Book 2: The Provence Series)*

Lauren is at a turning point. If only she knew *where* to turn. Her long-term relationship with Mark is fading fast. Instead, she feels drawn to Jean-Pierre, an attractive Frenchman she'd met the previous summer. When she's laid off from her job as a chef, she decides to go see him in Provence, France.

Mark can't get Lauren out of his heart, even though it's been close to a year since she asked him to give her space. When she goes to France, he's afraid he'll lose her for good. That is, until he decides to go there, too, as a last-ditch effort to win her back.

At first, Lauren is angry that Mark follows her to France. But a joint desire to help a young refugee boy leads them to work together. Lauren finds herself torn between the two men. Worse, she's confronted with obstacles in helping the boy and even greater obstacles within herself.

Kyle Hunter writes inspirational romance and women's fiction that sometimes take her characters to faraway places. She lived in France for thirteen years. Currently she lives in North Carolina where she also writes non-fiction (under the pen name K. B. Oliver) and teaches French.

Follow me on www.Kyle-Hunter.com

Goodreads

Bookbub

Amazon Author Page